Butcher Bird
Tales from Down Under

ISBN: 978-1-934582-72-5

LCCN: 2016948128

Published by Back Channel Press
Salem, NH, USA
Printed in the United States of America

Cover art and interior images by Matteo Grilli
www.matteogrilli.blogspot.com

Layout design and production by Deborah McKew

The following stories from this collection have been previously published in slightly different versions:

Piggy-wig (formerly entitled A Song) was published in Calliope, 1987

Monkey-eyes was published in Green Mountain Review, 1988

The Pink Wall was published in Confrontation, 1988

Trusting Games (formerly entitled Into the Silence) was published in Primavera, 1988

Cleaning Girls was published in Antipodes, the official journal of the American Association of Australasian Literary Studies, 1989

Currawongs was published in Louisville Review, 1989

Ellie was published in Great River Review, 1989

Severin's Gift was published in Green Mountain Review, 1989

Uncle Lawrence was published in Henniker Review, 1991

Such a Good Life (originally published under the title Hailstorm in Henniker Review, 1990) was published in Everyday Epiphanies, 1997

Monkey-eyes was submitted for the Pushcart Prize in 1988

To my family in the States:
my husband, Bill, and my children, Simon and Alison.

And, to my brothers Down Under:
Huon Marchmont and Justin Macquarie

Contents

Part One

The Farmhand 3

Butcher Bird 13

Hide and Come Seek 21

The Missionary 27

Annie's Song 35

Jake's All Night Open 40

Ellie 46

Trusting Games 52

Part Two

Monkey-eyes 60

Rhubarb Pie 67

Piggy wig 74

Home on the Night Train 79

Waiting for Queenie 86

Guv'ment Lady 93

The Pink Wall 100

A Flower for Malcolm 105

Part Three

Severin's Gift 117

Fallen Angels 121

Oolong Tea 131

Such a Good Life 140

A Complicated Case 146

Cleaning Girls 151

Uncle Lawrence 158

Free Flight 168

Dingo Lad 175

Currawongs 182

Part One

"Someone...once gave me a box full of darkness.
It took me years to understand
that this, too, was a gift."

Mary Oliver
The Uses of Sorrow, published in *Thirst*

The Farmhand

Madge Cummins rode her bike the three miles to Dave Hollings' farm. His water sprays were full on, twirling and spitting over the fields, and the wet leaves of the tomato plants glistened in the sun. She breathed in deep the warm, rich smell of the land. She propped her bike against the fence, and the cold spray hit her face. Surprised, she laughed out loud.

"You okay?" Hollings called. He was working between the rows of tomato plants.

She hadn't seen him crouched among the leaves. She wiped her cheeks and pressed back her hair. Hollings was dressed in khaki pants she recognized from the army surplus store on Market Street. His hat was set low on his forehead, his chin a white knob above the dark of his throat.

"You want something?" He settled back on his heels and stared at her.

"Eddie says you need someone can tie tomato plants," Madge said. Eddie Flint owned the only hotel in Mallee Downs and he knew where workers were needed.

Hollings stood up and pushed back his hat. "You done this work before?"

"Family had tomatoes," she said, though that was something of a lie. Her dad had never planted anything in his life, but their next door neighbor had a half-dozen tomato plants in pots, and she'd watched over the fence as he tended them.

"When do you want to start?" Hollings had a way of standing very still, his eyes floating over her, arms hanging by his sides.

It was Saturday and there was nothing to do in Mallee Downs on the weekend. Madge was tired of hanging out with her girlfriends at the local swimming hole where the boys flipped obscene fingers at them. They hooted and jeered, and got the hots watching the girls dive into the river or adjust the straps of their swimsuits. This summer she had discovered that the boys were still boys while she and her friends had become women.

Hollings' blue eyes seemed bright in their paleness. His eyes reminded Madge of Riki-Tiki-Tavi, the little mongoose she'd read about in sixth grade who stared down a cobra and eventually killed it. She'd loved that brave little mongoose, so she looked past Hollings, back to the gardens, the lush greenness flowing down to the river, the water droplets lit up by the sun.

"I can start today," she said.

Madge worked for him that Saturday, grubbing out the weeds from around the plants, tying up the loose tendrils, until her arms ached. Late afternoon she heard a two-note whistle, shrill enough to reach them at the end of the field. That would be Ethel Parsons, Hollings' live-in woman. Madge had heard she'd come to the farm five years ago after being laid off from the dry goods store; she worked in the fields and kept house. She had seen Ethel buying groceries at the shop, had seen her on the road sometimes walking to school, Ethel bumping by in a brown pickup truck. Madge longed to drive a truck, sitting high in the cab and away from the bulljoe ants, the dust, in a truck just like the one Ethel drove.

"You bring some grub?" Hollings asked.

"No." She was thirsty and sweat plastered her hair across her forehead. The juice from the tomato leaves covered her arms and hands, had caught under her nails, caught in the hairs of her wrists so they shone green.

"Come on up to the house then." He started off ahead of her, two rows separating them. The dirt swelled up and over her boots. They passed under the sprays and the water cooled her skin, ran green juice down her legs. She paused to take off her hat while Hollings slowed to wait for her.

Ethel Parsons was sitting on the back verandah. Brown-eyed. Full-breasted. Worn down. She wore a sleeveless cotton shift with front buttons, neck to hem. A six-pack of beer sat sweating on the small wooden table, its surface scrubbed so often it had a pearly sheen. A plate of buttered bread sat next to the beer. Madge could smell the yeasty richness of the vegemite spread.

"This's the Cummins girl," Hollings said as he sat down. "She wants to work this summer." He looked at Madge, his head cocked. "Right, love?"

Madge nodded.

Ethel stared at Hollings. "We don't need anyone, not this summer."

"We can always do with an extra pair of hands." He bit into the bread and Madge saw the space between his front teeth. "Give you a bit of a break," he grinned across the table at Ethel and swatted a fly off her shoulder.

"Break, be damned!" Ethel waved her beer in the air. "We've enough packers to see the season through. Dappy and Belle are enough in the fields. And they know what they're doing."

Hollings thumbed the top off a beer bottle. "Madge here needs some work, and she can tie. It'll give Dappy a chance to hoe the lettuce." Hollings raised the bottle. "You want one?" he asked Madge.

Madge took the beer; it was not her first one. She bit into the thick bread then drank thirstily. The day was cooling; the chattering starlings had quieted. She could see Dappy and Belle Miller walking slowly up through the tomato plants, their steps measured; they knew how to conserve energy.

"I'll drive you into town." Hollings said and turning to Ethel, asked, "You want anything at the store?"

Ethel shook her head. "Supper's at seven," she said. She didn't look at Madge.

Madge glanced at Hollings, old enough to be her father. He grinned at her and she liked the space between his front teeth, his slight lisp. When she'd thought of her future, she had hoped for something more than a strip of market garden, but land was land, and there weren't many choices for a girl in Mallee Downs. Heirloom tomatoes were beautiful: Brandywine Red, Black Krum, Druzba, Marglobe. Fifty acres of exotic sounding plants just had to make money.

Three weeks later, as Madge came out of the packing shed, washed up and ready to head home, she saw Ethel throwing two big suitcases into the back of the pickup.

"Where's Hollings?" Ethel asked.

"Back field," Madge replied. Was Ethel really leaving? Did Hollings know?

Ethel ran back up the house steps and came down carrying another carton. "Give me a hand," she pointed to the porch where a lamp and two small chairs waited.

"You going somewhere?" Madge asked.

"Damn right!" Ethel said.

Madge leaned her bike against the truck and fetched the chairs, went back for the lamp.

"I'll give you a lift into town if you're ready," Ethel said, settling the lamp beside the suitcases. The motor was running and the exhaust fumes, fanned by the breeze, wafted over them. "Throw your bike in the back."

Madge glanced back at the fields. If Hollings saw her helping Ethel run, would he blame her, maybe take her job away? And what would he do without his pickup truck?

"You did me a service," Ethel said as they jolted over the uneven road, "Coming here when you did."

Madge gripped the bar across the dashboard. The chairs bounced around in the back of the truck, dust flew off the wheels.

"You can have it." Ethel said, her eyes intent on the road. "Always something to hoe, something to pick, water pipes to be dragged around! Never ends! And the green stink!" Ethel gripped the steering wheel so hard her knuckles seemed huge. "Believe me, he's all promises and sweet talk, but never a ring."

Did Ethel think she was planning to marry Hollings? Madge wedged her knees firmly against the dashboard.

"Did you ever see me in a green dress, did you?" Ethel asked. "I wouldn't have green in the house—curtains, bedspread, pillows, not even a wash cloth. And Hollings stinks of that juice."

The truck bounced over the uneven dirt road.

"You know how old I am?" Ethel asked. "Not much older than you."

Madge saw how Ethel was slack under her dress, no waist to string a belt; her hands were knobby and thick. Madge tightened her seat belt, settled her hips on the seat.

"You think I was the first Hollings lived with, you're dead wrong," Ethel said as she pulled up in front of Madge's house. She waited while Madge hauled her bike off the truck and drove off in a wash of dust. Madge slept badly that night in her small bedroom; her father's snoring loud through the wall. In the morning her body was wrapped in the damp sheets.

Six weeks later, Hollings invited Madge to live in his house. He squared it with her parents, settling things with a weekly bag of heirloom tomatoes. Madge quickly learned his needs and those nights when they bucked and rocked together and her skin smelled of ripe green juice, Madge believed she could manage him and the farm.

The work in the fields was backbreaking. Hollings had planted a further acre of Black Truffles, but he had done less than usual, had relied more on her and the Millers and the boys who packed the tomatoes in the back shed. "Bloody knees have gone on me!" he complained at night. He'd been the local halfback in the Mallee Downs football team years ago but he'd spent more time facing the ground than he did running the field, though he told a different story when he got with his mates.

At the end of that summer they celebrated. The last of the tomatoes had been picked, the old vines pulled out ready for burning, the final cartons packed and sent to market. On Saturday a bonfire blazed in the near field, fueled by the pile of used stakes and dried greens. Hollings put his arm round her. The packing crew in their shorts and bare feet watched the flames shoot into the air while Dappy Miller, leaning against the shed wall with Belle by his side, watched her. Madge knew what they were all thinking, wondering how long she'd last before she loaded the pickup and left. She'd show them; she'd work harder than any of them; she knew what she was doing.

The next year, the busy season brought more plantings, more heat, more work. Madge was driving back to the farm in the early evening after leaving eighty-four cases of packed tomatoes at the rail junction for the Sydney markets. Mist was rising off the river when the red coat caught her eye: bright crimson in the headlights with the front edges flapping up from the wind.

Madge was tired. She didn't stop for hitchhikers, but the girl stared straight into the truck's lights, dumb and trusting, her thumb held high. Before she could lean over and push open the door, the girl was climbing into the cab. She looked about Madge's age only softer.

"Where're you going?" the girl asked, settling in the seat.

"Heading back to Mallee Downs," Madge said.

"Mallee Downs! Name sounds quiet." The girl stared through the front windscreen. "I'm looking for a town where things are quiet," she said.

She was small but her big, rounded carryall was full to bursting, and she held it with both hands tight against her belly.

"Any work round here?" the girl asked.

"Depends on what you can do," Madge said.

The girl leaned back in the corner of the cab and soon her head dropped to her chest. Everything in town was shut up tight except the Flint Hotel. Madge gave the girl a little shake.

"Yes," the girl said, her head snapping up. "We here?" she ran her fingers through her hair and massaged her neck.

"What can I call you," Madge asked. "In case you stay."

"Angie, Angie Madlow."

"Well, Angie, this is Flint's Hotel," Madge pointed at the lights in the windows. "You can put up here." The girl took her time getting down to the pavement, the big, soft bag in her hand. Madge wasn't going to stop but she could see Dappy Miller's head through the hotel window and she could check when he planned to finish the back field.

Flint's smelled of beer and tobacco smoke. Conversations stopped as they walked in and Madge saw the girl's coat was a darker red than it had appeared in the headlights.

"This is Angie Madlow," Madge announced to the three men in the room, Dappy Miller and his two mates. She turned to Eddie who was leaning on the bar. "You got an empty room?"

"Sure," he said, eyeing the girl. "How long you staying?"

"Haven't decided." Angie glanced up at the painting of Sassy Sal hanging above the long mirror running the length of the bar. Sal lay on her side, her flesh shining pinkly in the lights, one hand wedged coyly between her thighs, her other hand supporting her cheek. Sal looked down on Eddie's bald head with a little smile on her red lips, her eyes following him wherever he went.

"I can pay for a week," Angie said and leaned her bag against the bar.

The next morning, Madge stood over the griddle flipping pancakes and already sweating. Hollings came in and smacked her rear, held her waist with his big hands, nosed her neck. "Breakfast ready, love?"

Madge told Hollings about the girl in the red coat.

"You took her to Eddie's?" he asked, his lisp whistling through the gap in his front teeth

"Where else would I take her?" Madge slapped four pancakes down on his plate.

She finished stacking the dishes in the sink and left Hollings still eating, syrup coating the corners of his mouth.

"Get the pipes connected," he called after her. "I'll be right out."

Madge was adjusting to the day's brightness when she saw the girl leaning against the water tank, tight white T-shirt, grey cut-offs. Angie came toward her, a slow swing to her stride. "Mr. Flint told me you might need an extra pair of hands." She had her lunch wrapped in a white cloth: a large white hotel napkin Eddie must have given her. She was attractive in the daylight, large brown eyes under curved eyebrows, a wide mouth. No makeup.

"Sure is pretty here, Mrs. Hollings." She raised her hand to shade her eyes.

Mrs. Hollings! Madge could live for a time with someone who called her that. She heard Hollings coming up behind her, kicking up the dust. "This the hitchhiker?" he asked.

Madge nodded.

Hollings looked at Angie, and Madge saw him eyeing her the way he'd eyed Madge when she first came to the farm, arms dangling at his sides, hat shading his eyes. "How long you staying?"

Madge knew they could use some help. The plants were sprouting more leaves and shoots, climbers hanging down off the last ties they'd done a week ago, shoots ready to snap if the wind lifted them. "No point starting work," Madge said, cutting through the heat, "then leaving."

"I need money to move on," Angie said, talking past Madge to Hollings.

"She can do some tying," Hollings said. "Dappy can train her."

Madge looked across at the Millers as they moved between the rows, bending and stretching, both in step, either side of the plants. They'd been doing this work so long they looked like they were dancing together. With another person they could finish tying in two days instead of three, hoeing could be finished the following week.

"Why don't you go into town?" Hollings nudged Madge in the back. "You know I can't work that damn clutch with these knees." He slapped his thighs to emphasize the fact. "Pick up the fertilizer, love. I'll change the pipes for you. Show Angie, here, 'round the place." He gestured to Angie and they walked off down the path, Hollings leading the way.

At lunch break, Angie came up to wash, her arms and hands stained dark green. She smelled of tomato juice, like they all did: an overpowering pungency. Her T-shirt was stained and her feet through the sandals were dusty-green. Hollings had connected an old tub up to the water pipe at the side of the house. Hollings washed first. He carried the water to his face in his cupped hands, swooshed it once, twice, three times before he wiped his face in the towel. Angie did the same, making bubbling sounds as she washed the green film off her cheeks, her lips. Taking up the linen napkin from her lunch, she wiped her face and laughed as the white cloth stained green. "Sure hope Mr. Flint can get these stains out," she said.

Angie sat with the Millers at the picnic bench off in the shade. Hollings and Madge sat on the verandah, the six-pack in front of him, sandwiches within arm's length. They didn't talk, nothing to catch up on, and as they ate Madge watched Hollings sneak glances at Angie.

Madge remembered how she had arrived that sun-filled day; Hollings taking her round the farm, explaining farm work in that cozy way he had, every question she asked taken seriously. She'd learned to tie those plants quickly, learned to swing the hoe, drive the tractor, haul up the water pipes.

Angie looked ready to learn, too.

In the months that followed, the tomatoes flourished, were picked over, grew some more and were picked over again. The season looked good. There were the usual interruptions: the small tractor blew a gasket; the connection in one of the water pipes broke; Belle caught the flu. And as the weeks passed, Angie found a rhythm. She moved gracefully between the rows, sure-footed in the loose soil, the bundle of green string slipped under her belt where she nimbly pulled a length as needed.

Late summer, Madge sat on the edge of the bed. She'd waited long enough to see if Hollings brought up the subject of marriage again. He'd told her she was the one, the one he'd been waiting for, the one he wanted to marry back on her birthday.

"I want an answer, Hollings," she said. "Summer's almost over. I want us to be legal."

Hollings came back from the bathroom, tying the cord on his pajama pants. "Wouldn't you just," he replied. "You've got a roof over your head, food on the table." He laughed and put a hand on her thigh. "You got everything," he said. "Don't rock the boat."

"What happens if you keel over? Where do I go then?" Madge sat straighter. "What happens to the farm?" He was a cripple, a gap-toothed old fool, but she'd come to love his land. Not just need it, but love it. She pulled her nightshirt over her knees.

Hollings slid into bed, rolled on to his side and pulled the sheets his way. "It's all settled, you and me," he said. "Go to sleep!"

Madge turned to the wall and held the wind-dried sheet across her mouth. Lately he had her doing daily errands: delivering the tomato cartons to the rail station, picking up bales of string, lugging the fertilizer, filling the cans with gasoline for the tractor. She was like Ethel, riding high in the cab of the truck with another woman at home no more than three steps behind him wherever he went. And Angie was looking like one of the sweeter heirloom tomatoes, ripe for picking, maybe picked already.

The next morning Madge slipped the dirty breakfast dishes into the sink.

"You'll need to move the water pipes again," Hollings said as he pushed back his chair.

Madge glanced out the window. She didn't want to look into those pale eyes of his. He'd become the Riki-Tiki-Tavi in the story and she knew what happened in the end. The mongoose killed the snake and they both died. There was no lasting security for her here, no legal papers; no ring on her finger. She should have listened to Ethel, planned ahead.

"Get Angie to do them." She watched Hollings pause on the back verandah and survey his land, the rolling lushness. "I've got things to do in the house."

Madge looked round the kitchen, the living room, and there was nothing else she wanted to take with her. Her suitcase was packed and waiting behind the kitchen door. She'd be traveling light. She grabbed the keys for the pickup and checked that Hollings was out of sight. The suitcase landed on a pile of empty tomato cartons, some metal pipe connectors. She released the brake and revved the engine. The clutch on this new truck just suited her fine.

Butcher Bird

Laura Nelson unpacked her few clothes and hung them in the small bedroom closet. She caught sight of her face in the mirror above the dressing table, the winged shape of her eyebrows so like her daughter's it was difficult to look in mirrors anymore. She regretted that Saturday when, before it was light, Sally had called from the bedroom door. "Wake up, Mummy! We have to get the balloons!" It was the weekend, there was plenty of time, and she had scolded her daughter for waking her so early.

The air in the bedroom smelled of camphor and floor polish, a dusty spider web hung in the corner of the room, the candlewick bedspread reached the floor. Laura missed the lights of the city, the sounds of traffic, television voices murmuring through walls, but friends had urged her to use their holiday cottage. "You're too thin!" they'd said. "Take a long weekend." And Marshall had agreed. As though they both suffered a chronic illness, she and her husband had learned this past year to be very kind, very caring of each other.

There was a bottle of sherry in the kitchen cabinet, and Laura returned with her glass to sit by the open window in the bedroom. The house next door had its porch light on and it was comforting to know someone lived close by. What had their friends said? "Say 'hello' to Amos when you see him, he's our caretaker and neighbor, a nice man."

The pine forest at the back of the cottage stretched beyond the window frame, and she listened to the wind soughing through the branches. There were small flashes of white between the trees, not the flash of fireflies, but something more substantial, and as she strained to see in the darkness she heard the lone bird call again, those same high notes, full and clear, like the tapping of crystal bells.

She held the glass tightly. Her fingers were long and smooth, her wide gold band loose between her knuckles. Laura could still see the helium balloons tied to the birthday chair. She and Marshall had waited eight long years to have a child, and then Sally arrived, their beautiful daughter. Every year they celebrated and after Sally's last birthday, after the party was over, Laura had gone inside to tidy up. She was clearing the last of the food off the kitchen table when the neighbor's child ran into the house crying, "Sally won't leave the water. She won't play anymore."

Laura had laughed and reminded the child not to get her clothes wet. The pond was shallow, with water lilies at one end and three fat goldfish that surfaced to eat their bread crusts. It was something in the way the child continued to stand there, repeating "Sally won't play," that made her run to the patio where the remains of the party littered the lawn and a cluster of bright balloons flew from the birthday chair.

Later, Marshall asked her, "How could it happen? Where were you?" his voice breaking. "How could Sally drown in two feet of water?"

"She must have slipped." Laura was numb. There were still birthday presents to be opened, thank-you notes to be written. "The moss was wet. The stones…"

The next morning, Laura checked out the cottage in more detail, grateful for the electricity that ran the lights and antiquated stove, the sparse furniture, the neatness of the rooms. Outside, the paving stones were uneven, the garden overgrown. She walked past clumps of daisies and geraniums and a jungle of cotoneasters. Perhaps in the few days she had at the cottage she could bring some order to this neglect.

A sharp smack split the air. Across the dividing fence her neighbor was working, cutting wood with easy swings of his axe. A little girl sat on a stump to the side, watching him. Her blonde hair covered her face; her thin arms were clasped around her knees. Lengths of cut wood were neatly stacked around them, walls of textured arcs and curves, sharp triangles. Her

14

friends had forgotten to mention that Amos had a daughter.

Laura turned aside and set to work. She trimmed the weeping crab apple, staked the hydrangea, cleared the side bed of thistles. She worked until only the sound of the bees filled her thoughts. In the late afternoon, while Laura was resting, she heard her neighbor call.

"Anyone home?"

Laura put aside her book and opened the door. Amos stood inside the fence. The sunburned dome of his head shone and his beard glistened with water drops. The child stood a little distance from him, fiddling with a handful of wild daisies. Her legs looked like two brown sticks beneath her brief summer dress.

"Hallo," he called when he saw her. "Got everything you need?" He beckoned for the child to come closer, and she leaned against his leg. "The neighbors let me know you'd be here." He grinned. "I thought you might join me for an evening drink." He pointed in the general direction of his house. "It's so warm the local fireflies should put on a performance tonight. We can watch them from the verandah." The child dropped some of the flowers and bent to pick them up.

"This is my daughter." Amos touched the child's shoulder. "Say hello, Jess." She moved from under his hand, preoccupied with arranging the daisy stems into a posy.

"Hallo, Jess," Laura smiled but there was no eye contact, no gesture of greeting. The child's hair veiled her face. When she didn't answer, Laura hesitated.

Amos shrugged and looked off. "Maybe another time."

"No, no," she said, "it's kind of you to ask. Let me get my shawl."

It was hanging off the hall chair, a gift from Marshall the night she packed. After she'd opened the box, he'd lifted the shawl, soft and grey, and draped it round her shoulders, fumbling to loop the ends over her breasts. "Keep warm," he'd said. And she'd thanked him.

They crossed the yard and passed single file through the gate. Amos straightened chairs on the verandah and moved a large pot of parsley off the small table to the floor.

"They told me." Amos brushed away the dried parsley fronds. "A terrible tragedy."

Laura sat down at the cleared table. "Thank you," she said. "You're very kind." She had learned that politeness was the easiest response.

"You'll have a whiskey?" he asked and disappeared inside.

Jess leaned against the outside rail, her shoulder blades sharp through her summer dress. She plucked the heads from the daisy stems, one by one, and threw them on the ground.

Laura accepted the glass Amos brought out and held it up against the waning light. "When I was unpacking last night," she said, "I saw something white moving around in the pines up there."

Amos laughed. "Old Donovan's ghost, perhaps, he lived here a long time ago. My Gran would tell me stories about him, about how he came back to turn the pine needles at night searching for his buried gold."

"Gold?" Laura smiled. "In a pine forest?"

"Back then I believed her." Amos crossed his legs. "Thought I'd find the gold and we'd all live happily ever after." He looked over at Jess, who was pacing round a shrub, arms spread like a bird. "It's a story for children. You probably saw Jess up there, she loves playing in the pines. Her dressing gown is white."

Sally had chosen a white dress for her birthday party, a red sash at her waist and red ribbons in her hair. "You live here with Jess?" Laura asked, "Just the two of you?" Images of a white dress slipping between trees, of children drowning in pine needles, of red ribbons caught in lily stems, came to Laura. *Let it go*, she told herself, taking a quick sip of whiskey.

"Kristen's not happy in the country. She's a lawyer and needs to be in the city. She visits twice a month." He waved his hand toward the child. "It's better this way, and Jess is happy here."

She and Marshall had lived apart after the accident—in different bedrooms, eating at different tables, passing each other quietly in the hall. They touched, gentle pats on an arm or a cheek that came to serve in place of words. They were sensible people. Ultimately, they reasoned, no one was to blame.

Jess had gone to the shed and came out carrying a large paper bag. She sat cross-legged on the grass, pulled a fat yellow hamster from the bag, and cradled it in her lap. "That's Sammy *the Third.*" Amos said. "We keep the local pet store in business."

Laura watched as the hamster climbed on the child's knee and was returned to her lap. Again and again. If Jess was her daughter she'd have the best specialists in the country involved. She gripped the armrest, it was all so unfair. How could Sally, bright and intelligent, with her whole life before her, be taken?

Amos stood up. "Look!" he walked to the railing. "Look, Jess! The fireflies!"

In the growing darkness tiny pricks of light flashed out a hundred changing patterns. Jess darted among them. She began to dance, spinning, arms spread, skirt flaring round her bare legs.

Amos watched his daughter and smiled. Jess was oblivious, a whirling dervish. She rounded the corner of the shed and was gone.

"Wasn't that something?" Amos asked.

"The fireflies were wonderful," Laura pulled the shawl closer. She couldn't bear the sight of his happiness. If only Marshall had left his all-consuming job for Sally's party it might not have happened; if only she hadn't gone in to clean up the kitchen, she'd have been there when Sally fell. The birthday party was over, everyone had gone home. Sally and her little friend from next door were just going to feed the goldfish.

Saturday passed quickly. Laura walked into the village along the track where the ghost gums met overhead. She bought some milk and eggs and a ham sandwich for lunch and exchanged nods with the few townspeople she passed. On her way home she picked some sprays of native boronia, long untidy stems of maroon flowers, from along the side of the road.

The wildflowers had been in full bloom the day she and Sally went to see the hot-air balloons lift off from Macquarie Field. They arrived late because of traffic, and by the time they parked the car the first balloons had risen against the backdrop of the trees. More balloons rose, at least a dozen, listing a little before settling into the wind currents. Sally's face was flushed with excitement and she'd tugged Laura's hand. "Look," she whispered, "they don't make a sound." She pulled Laura toward a balloon still stretched out on the ground, watched as it slowly inflated. "Wait, Mummy, soon it will fly." They watched as it filled with hot air, the flames flickering up into the body of the balloon, the basket bouncing a little on the ground, until it rose like a picture-book drawing against the bank of white clouds.

Laura pushed the boronia's woody stems into the white enamel jug on the table and put the milk away. She ate the sandwich with a cup of tea and went outside to read. The tulip tree was dropping its flowers, large pinkish-red petals that stained everything they touched. She brushed them carefully off her chair. It was peaceful, quiet. She saw Amos carry an armful of wood into the house, and later, she waved to Jess, who stood at the dividing fence, rigid as a young sapling on a still day.

The next morning, her last day, Laura walked through the pine forest and on her return met Amos at the fence.

"You should be in bare feet," he said. "Feel the pine needles firsthand."

"I've forgotten how to walk without shoes." She said. She remembered the bird, how it came to the tulip tree in the early evening, and described its call.

"A butcher bird," he told her. "There's a pair of them here, plain grey things but their call is beautiful."

"Butcher bird?" Laura reached for the fence. "What an ugly name."

"They have to live, too." Amos laughed, oblivious to the look on Laura's face. "Funny thing is, they kill small birds and hang them on a branch to eat later." He moved along the fence and opened the gate for her. "Jess found a dead blue wren the other day and wrapped it in her blanket to warm it." He smiled at Laura. "She thought she could bring it back."

Feathers and beaks, goldfish and water lilies. Sally's blonde hair had floated on the water, the long red hair ribbon resting below the surface. When Laura heaved her daughter's small body from the ornamental fishpond and cradled her, the puffy eyelids remained closed. The lump on Sally's forehead was mottled and blue.

That afternoon, while Laura was reading under the tulip tree, Jess came through the gate. She stopped a short distance from Laura's chair and began raking the fallen flowers together with her fingers. She finished shaping the mound, stood silently, and gazed at Laura.

"That's lovely, Jess," Laura said. "We can build a fairy house." Laura moved her chair aside. She and Sally had made fairy houses in their backyard. Sally chose stones for paths and put white daisy heads in for windows; she made chimneys and fences to keep the cows out.

Laura built the mound higher. "There should be a door here," Laura made a depression with her fist. "Can you find some stones to make a path, Jess?"

Jess didn't move. Laura looked up at her. "Please, Jess, some little stones?"

The child kicked Laura's hand. She kicked again and stamped on the house of petals, ground her heels in them until the red juice bled into her dusty feet. She whirled around and knocked over Laura's chair, spilling books and reading glasses.

"You're spoiling it!" Laura cried. Jess made a high, moaning sound in her throat.

Laura reached for the child's arm. Jess spat and Laura felt the spittle land on her cheek. "Jess, stop it!" Laura demanded. She caught the child's dress and tugged. "Stop it now!" This wasn't the same child who danced with the fireflies.

"Jess!" Amos was at the fence. "Come home, Jess, time to wash up."

Jess ignored her father and kicked again, her foot connected painfully with Laura's thigh. Laura let go the skirt and raised her hand. Before she understood what she was doing her hand fell, and she heard the sharp smack as it connected with the child's bare leg. God, she had never hit Sally, ever. The red mark deepened to the star-shape of her palm. How could this be happening?

The child scooped up a handful of flowers and threw them at Laura's head.

Amos called again. This time Jess heard her name and ran across the lawn to her father, who swung her up against his chest. She pounded his shirt with her fists. Amos held her tight. "Jess came to say good-bye," he said quietly, and shifted his daughter to his hip.

Laura rose to her feet. "I'm so sorry," she stood by the overturned chair. "I wanted to play with her." She wiped the spit from her cheek.

"Jess doesn't know much about playing," Amos carried Jess effortlessly.

"I didn't realize…" Laura felt tears stinging her eyes.

"Have a safe trip home," Amos called at the gate.

Inside the cottage, Laura washed her hands and face. The spit mingled with the tears. She could still feel the impact of her hand on the child's leg; the first time she had touched a child since Sally had drowned. The balloons had been so beautiful flying above the birthday chair. Marshall should have been there to see them lift.

She emptied the wilted flowers into the trash can, watched as the blossoms floated a little before falling. Sally had tugged on her arm that birthday morning and said, "I love these balloons, Mummy. Sophia and Addie will come and we'll play. It will be such fun!"

Laura packed her suitcase and pulled the shawl around her shoulders, looping the ends together just as Marshall had done the night before she left. She poured a glass of sherry, opened the bedroom window, and stared into the dark wall of pines. She searched for the ghosts of little girls darting freely among the tree trunks and heard the butcher bird's call, clear-sounding, like crystal bells released. Laura realized, in that moment, she could begin to share the details of this weekend with Marshall.

Hide and Come Seek

In the den, Lou gives one of his two-note whistles. "Did you see that?" he yells. The voice of the TV commentator rises and the stadium crowd roars again.

"We'll wait for the replay." I hear Vinnie say, "Too close to call."

"Who needs a replay?" Lou asks. "He was in by two feet."

"Go on," Frank replies. "He crossed the sideline. One foot over. He'll be called on that."

"He was in," Lou says, "Rose, we need more beer from the fridge!"

His mates have come for the big one, the Rugby Grand Final. Lou sits in his easy chair and tips the back down until the footrest comes up. He's allowed the last word on each play. It's his house, his and mine, though he and his mates won't have me in the den anymore. Not a woman's thing, they say. In the past I rooted for Pennant Hills, the one Lou bet on to lose, and they turned round and won. Twelve years we've been married and he's never forgotten. That's the way it is between us—them in there with their games, and me in the kitchen waiting on them. I've got the daily crossword spread out on the table. The fridge is full of snacks for halftime, the beer is ice-cold, but I can't settle.

Lou says I foul things up. They're the experts. "You just try the long odds, the lucky shots," he says. "That's not following the game right." He doesn't know I have to be careful with games. I find them unpredictable. I may think I'm following the play right, then the rules change and I'm into something completely different.

Take the game of tag. He played tag as a kid, like I did, out on a playground neatly contained on a square of yard. We went to a small, one-room school filled with kids in all grades so lunch hour was break-out time. Playing tag, I was always caught by the boy with a shock of black hair, long arms wrapping my chest and his body pressing into mine, while I struggled and he wouldn't let go. Lou doesn't understand—he thinks games are logical. He's great at games; he's played them all his life.

Last Friday Lou was talking about football as usual. I broke in and talked about the film I saw Wednesday night. It was about a fellow in Brazil who's flying off in his mind, flew with wings glistening white like he'd just been hatched, free as some over-sized eagle. He was dying all the time from being tortured. That shook me, him nearly dead yet living his life like it was happening now. I thought, that man is free. I tried to explain that part of it, and he said, "It's all make-believe, Rose."

"No, it wasn't," I snapped. "You talk about football and pennants all the time. That film was as real as any Rugby final." I take my films seriously. You could call me a film buff, catching all the Saturday matinees I can while they're watching their games. Popcorn and soda, and when the lights go out, I'm lost in the story. I'm free.

"Rose," he said, his face serious. "Stop daydreaming for once."

"Don't tell me what's real or not," I said. "Some things are more real than you could imagine."

"You're floating again," Lou said, "in Never-Never land." He laughed.

At that moment I could have flipped off the TV and thrown it out the window, along with him and the remote control.

For some reason today, I'm ready for Lou. I know he enjoys games. I can't complain he's down at the pub drinking away the evening with his mates. No way. They're middle-aged now so they're all in the gym, Lou, Vinnie, Bob and Frank, sweating around the handball courts, headbands clinging to their foreheads, damp wristbands, knee supports.

"Rose!" he calls again from the den. "Where's the six-pack?"

I grab the beer off the shelf and slam the fridge door. If Lou wants his beer he should come and get it but I know there's no way he'll leave his chair.

"By God, he's made it, he's in!" Frank's voice is full of potato chips. "I tell you boys, that was sweet!"

"We need a toast!" Bob's come alive at last.

Vinnie calls, "Hey, Rose-love, you got some more of the wet stuff?"

"Rose, what's keeping you out there?" Lou has the final word.

"Hold on," I yell. "I'm getting the pretzels." I tip them out on a plastic plate and throw some sweet gherkins on the side for Vinnie and the plate tips sideways.

There is laughter and clapping from the den. Their team has scored.

"Rose!" Lou's voice pushes up and over Vinnie's laughter.

"Relax!" Frank says. "She's coming!"

I'm holding the beer in one hand and I bend to pick up the food scattered on the floor. Outside the kitchen window Balch Mountain rises and I see a bird, wings spread, coasting on the thermals. You want your beer, Lou? You want to play games? I'll give you a game. Catch me. The words form in my head; I like the phrase. "Catch me," I whisper and the words balloon into the kitchen, past the cupboards that need painting. "Catch me, Lou." I say aloud while the TV commentators call a thirty-yard carry and I'm off and running through the house.

The hall is darker than usual, with the trees near the window raising shadows on the walls. Shadow people. The stairs are ahead. And it's up, like in those old movies where the bad guy goes up to the roof, feet clattering on the metal steps, his mouth open, sucking in his last breath. The good guys come on with their guns drawn, baggy pants flapping, sweat on their brows. They can be noisy; they're in charge of the outcome, and we know what happens—the bad guy gets caught. Though it's not as simple as that; being caught is never simple.

Are those footsteps behind me? I climb the stairs quickly, run silently on the carpeted floor to the bedrooms—ours and the spare, beds neatly made. There are no closets to hide in, no bed to crawl under; the window is latched, no chance of escape. Do his footsteps fall silent on the stairs? He'll check the hallway. He'll look in the bedrooms, in all the places he thinks I might hide, breathing hard while he concentrates.

In the bathroom there's only the shower, its curtain splashed with huge purple iris, blades of olive-green leaves. But no one hides behind shower curtains anymore—not after the movie, that crazy guy with his knife and the wide-open eye. The wicker basket sits in the angle of the wall hidden beyond the shower recess. I stand on the lid and the bamboo strains under my weight. I'm not sure if it can hold me; my feet might go through the lid like some pratfall in an old black-and-white, a Laurel and Hardy maybe, so I stand there, hands hiding my face and wait.

"Rose!" Lou's calling through the walls. "Bring in the beer!"

I look out through the window. Balch Mountain is there; it's always there. Lou argued about putting such a large window in the bathroom. "Stupid," he said. "All that cold air against a huge sheet of glass makes the heating bill rise." But this window keeps me going. I see right up Balch Mountain to the very top where the she-oak pines are thick. I could walk across them—just stand on the sill and step off, fly down through the valley where the water is clear to the sand.

The door squeaks softly. I feel the tiny movement of air from where I'm standing, like breath from a baby's mouth. We didn't have babies, Lou and me, though we worked at it for years. Still, I know what baby's breath would feel like on my cheek. Like that woman whose baby got taken by dingoes, out in the desert, lost baby's breath.

But nothing happens. It sounds like the bathroom door is closing. I'm all alone, Queen of the Mountain. He didn't think of me perched on the basket of clothes, in clear sight if he'd walked to the window. He'll find me though. He's done it before when he wants something—his winning team's cap or an old sweatshirt; he goes back to the places he's searched. He'll search all night if he has to. He loves games and he loves winning, against anyone, even me. He especially likes winning in the house—first to get up, first for the paper, last word in an argument. Always winning!

"Rose!" Lou yells, and the light snaps off on Balch Mountain.

I'm standing by the fridge with the six-pack in my hand and I'm holding my breath like a kid caught in some lie. The pretzels and gherkins are on the floor and the guys are calling. I reach for more pretzels.

"Come on, love," Vinnie calls again. "The game will be over before we blow the froth from the Toohey's!"

"Rose! For God's sake!" Lou's standing in the kitchen doorway. "Where the hell is our six-pack?" He sounds like a commercial before the main attraction. All beer, cars and football!

"You're missing the play, Lou," Frank yells over a Chevy commercial. One of the guys laughs and I hear the crackle of an empty potato chip bag being balled up in someone's hands.

"It's all yours, Lou!" I say, as I shove the beer against his chest. "Take the pretzels, Lou."

"Wait a minute," he says.

"That's it, Lou. No more games." I pull the sleeves of my sweater down to my wrists.

"You talking about football, love?" He's holding the pack of beer and plate of pretzels tightly in his hands as though his life depended on them.

"Quit daydreaming, Lou." I've raised my voice and I don't care if his mates hear us or not. "You don't even see me anymore."

Vinnie is standing in the doorway, grinning. Lou looks over at him, "Rose has gone crazy," he says.

"You crazy, Rose?" Vinnie takes the six-pack out of Lou's hands and pulls a bottle out for himself. "You should talk to Bev. She's crazy, too." He flips the top off and takes a drink. "I tell her, hang in there, it's the end of the season."

They laugh together as they go back to the den.

I sweep the spilled pretzels into the garbage and I'm back on my knees wiping up the gherkin juice on the floor with a paper towel. I don't hear Lou's voice anymore.

I walk up the stairs. The afternoon sun has gone and there are no distant shadows. The bedroom is a mess. I walk by the doorway and turn into the bathroom. The wicker basket is there, the lid wedged open by the leg of Lou's jeans. The plastic shower curtain needs replacing. The big purple iris looks faded and the curtain is torn at the side where Lou pulls it back each time he steps over the tub.

"Rose," Lou's calling from downstairs. "The guys are leaving. We won!"

I think about the guy in the film who made himself over, huge wings and all, dying he dreamed another place and kept living. If he came to this window right now I'd follow him to Balch Mountain, play tag in the wind without rules.

"Hey, Rose! You up there?"

The Missionary

Rachel Foote straightened before the small square organ at St. John's Church, her hands firm on the opening chords, her black Mary Jane's pumping the pedals until the floorboards vibrated. How could she go on like this, waiting for George Kettering. Three years and not a word from him! Her own father had died before she knew him in the Great War, at Gallipoli. Should she expect George to return when her father had not?

Rachel moved her sleeve against the wetness in her armpit. She was weary of war talk, of this never-ending drought. She needed a paper fan like those she saw fluttering among the pews while Reverend Dodd consoled his parishioners. "...suffering the worst heat wave in memory," he said. "...families watch their crops die, suffer with the families who lost homes to bush fires. We must have faith..." The parishioners bowed their heads.

Rachel completed the final refrain and the hall emptied quickly. She draped her mother's blanket across the box-shaped organ and wrapped the sunburned dahlias from the altar for the Reverend to take to the next service, counted the offering and wrote the amount neatly on the corner of the brown envelope.

Every Sunday she played the church organ like her mother before her. She slept through the weekday afternoons so she could work for the phone company at night. In the small back room of the Post Office, with the fan on high, she connected people to a world outside her small town. She prayed for a change, for a new direction in her life. When she joined the women on Monday mornings in the Rectory they asked questions over their teacups, "Have you heard nothing?" they asked with a gentle pat on her arm. "No word has come yet from George?"

The Kettering farm lay twenty miles out of town, wheat fields scorched by the heat, gardens burned. When Dave Kettering died, his wife, Ida, had donned his work shirt and pants and kept the farm going—for herself, and for George when he came home.

Rachel's hot cheeks told it all. "Sad, so sad, his mother's waiting, too. And the farm, this drought…?"

She and George had grown up in the town, gone to school together. There had been no promises made between them, but three years ago George had brushed his lips to her cheek at the Christmas Frolic. Weeks later, at the railway station with his army pack hanging off his shoulder, he'd called to her, "Don't forget me!"

The wisteria vine beside the porch, planted by her mother years ago to conceal the square lines of the house, was over-grown, choking the entrance-way. Rachel put her shoes neatly inside the door, opened the neck of her dress one button. In the kitchen, she made a sandwich and a hot cup of tea, then she lay down on the neatly folded counterpane and thought of the missionary couple from New Guinea. Their sermon was the only one in memory that had thrilled her. Was this a sin, Rachel wondered, to expect a calling, to wish for a sign? Rachel's mother had known her place. She returned from church each Sunday to sit at her small Berlioz upright in the living room, replaying hymns from morning matins, practicing for evensong, agonizing over the chords. On her last Sunday, after the pneumonia had taken hold, she'd bundled up in layers of wool, her blue plaid coat tugging at its buttons, and murmured, "You understand, Rachel, I have a calling." Her mother's burial brought out the whole town.

Six months after her mother's funeral, Rachel boarded the train to Sydney. She had gone only three times in her life and now she was traveling suburban streets in a taxi, past an open park where a deserted playground stood beside a graveyard, by rows of terraced houses and scruffy pepper trees.

The door of the missionary's house was flaking blue paint. She used the iron knocker above the sign reading: *Hawkers and Canvassers need not Call.* Was she doing the right thing, coming like this, without contacting them ahead of time? The door opened and Mr. Sutton appeared above her. "Who do you want?" he asked.

"Mr. Sutton, I'm Rachel Foote from Kurrajong. Last year you spoke at our church." Her lips were dry. "About New Guinea, and working there."

"In Kurrajong?" She saw him look at her worn shoes, taking in the lines of her face. "You were the organist, I remember now." He stepped back and smiled. "Come all the way from the country to visit, have you?"

"Who is it, Marty?" A woman's voice called from inside the house.

"A young lady from the church in Kurrajong! Months ago. Upcountry!"

"Tell her to come in!" There was a thump then the shuffle of slippered feet.

Rachel sat on the over-stuffed lounge while Mr. Sutton settled among the pile of newspapers on his chair, sending some to the floor. A big orange cat jumped up on his lap and he stroked its fur. Rachel didn't like cats. She suffered from allergies, could feel her throat tightening.

"You've travelled a long way, dearie, I'll put on the kettle." Mrs. Sutton gathered up the newspapers at her husband's feet. The front of her slippers had been cut out to make room for her toes. Another cat, this one a tabby, grey and black, pushed past Mrs. Sutton's legs and landed on the back of Rachel's chair. The cat's tail flicked back and forth, skimming her hair.

Mrs. Sutton returned with a tray. "Now tell us why you've come, dearie." The hem of her dress hung down untidily making one leg look shorter than the other. She sat down and wound her fat braid of white hair into a circle on top of her head and pinned it in place.

"I want to go as a missionary," Rachel declared. "Like you."

"No one wants to do missionary work anymore." Mrs. Sutton placed her tea cup on the table. "New Guinea? It happened a long time ago, didn't it, Marty?"

"We were young, Elizabeth." Mr. Sutton spoke to his wife as though Rachel was not there. "We've got the good memories yet, a chance to pass those on." The orange cat jumped down from his lap and headed for the door. "We were strong in our faith."

Rachel was having trouble breathing.

"I lost my baby and you praised the Lord I was spared." Her voice, fierce for a moment, faltered. "It was so long ago, dearie." She lifted her teacup and drained it. "There are some things shouldn't be put into words."

"We built huts, watched over the sick," Mr. Sutton's voice rose.

"Now then, Marty, she doesn't want to hear a sermon." Mrs. Sutton stacked the tea cups and looked at Rachel. "Nowadays, people want miracles more than the truth."

Rachel called at the Rectory the following week. The Reverend Dodds filled his pipe, slowly tamping down the tobacco with his forefinger. "The Sutton's? Nice people." He felt in his pocket for matches. "And Sydney? You had quite an adventure!"

Rachel relaxed into the chair cushions. She leaned on the Reverend's words just as her mother had done through the years.

"Did seeing the Sutton's help?" The match head flared and the sweet smell of Woodbine filled the room.

"I didn't realize their service in New Guinea happened so long ago. I thought they were there now." Rachel ran her fingers round the velvet paisley pattern on the chair's arm. "I thought I might go with them."

"You really want to leave Kurrajong?" The smoke drifted up from his pipe. "Your mother just gone."

She smoothed her hair back and replaced the tortoiseshell clips. "I think I do, yes!"

"Have you heard about George Kettering?" The Reverend asked abruptly. "He's been in a French hospital. He'll be coming home soon."

"George? Coming home?" Why hadn't Ida Kettering contacted her? Rachel pulled on her summer gloves, smoothing the fabric over each finger. "He's never written," she said as she moved to the door.

"You don't have to leave town to do the Lord's work." Reverend Dodd took her arm gently and turned her to face him. "While you're waiting, I wonder if you could help a woman in town, her husband left her with two little boys. Just a few hours a day, maybe twice a week; working with her might reveal a calling."

Rachel hurried toward the small house leaning on its foundation, piles of junked metal stacked round the yard. Broken toys and an upended tricycle lay near the front steps and she could see the boys hiding in the cabin of the abandoned truck. Six weeks of coming to this place had worn her duty thin, whittled away the hope of changing anything. Beryl was slouched against the door frame. "You got here," she said. She'd wrapped her head in a dull red scarf but strands of unwashed hair escaped round her broad, pale forehead.

Rachel shoved her hands deeper into her coat pockets for warmth. The house was bleak, sparsely furnished; the one bright note was the flutter of curtains in the single front window. She'd made the curtains during her first week there and hung them while Beryl watched from the middle of the room. "Nice," Beryl had said folding her arms. "Making extra work for me, washing them."

Rachel threw the empty soup cans into the garbage pail, careful of the cock-eyed lids with their barbed sharpness. Beryl settled her weight in a kitchen chair and lit a cigarette. "Running out of wood again!" she said, blunt like the stroke of an axe. Her face was turned to the kitchen door, the approaching autumn chill. "Don't know where to get it now. Him just leaving the way he did, nothing planned."

"Get it at Bernie's." Rachel scooped up the bits of food that floated to the surface of the sink water. "You know what to do; we've been through this before."

Beryl lit one cigarette from the tip of the other. "Easy for you to tell me what to do, with only yourself to worry about."

Rachel stacked the dishes on the open shelf beside the bottles of nail polish, every shade of red. "You could get a job. Bernie says he could do with some help on Saturdays."

"And no one to mind the kiddies." The skin on her neck hung in loose folds. Her cardigan dragged across her chest.

Rachel took up the broom and attacked the twists and scraps that lay around the corners of the stove. "Get the mop, Beryl. You can do the floor while I get some lunch."

Beryl moved heavily to the door. The elegance of her feet surprised

Rachel. They were long and slim in the rubber flip-flops, her toenails painted a bright cherry red.

The boys appeared with their clothes hanging untidily on their limbs. "We're hungry!" It was the oldest boy who spoke, the younger one hovering behind.

"Just wait til I'm done!" Beryl dumped the bucket on the floor, twirling the mop like a peasant woman grinding grain.

"The organ-player'll make them." The older boy pointed at Rachel.

She found the bread, the vegemite, the wilted lettuce and made them sandwiches. She and Beryl leaned against the sink while the boys took the two chairs, drumming their feet against the table legs. The curtains moved in the westerly breeze. In the six weeks of service, Beryl and the boys had not changed, but she had. There was no calling for her here.

Rachel played the organ on her last Sunday service. The upturned faces of the congregation waited patiently for the last amen. They welcomed the thought of the roast slow-baking in the oven at home, potatoes browning, treacle pudding warmed on the stove top. The drought had broken. The air was cooling. The war in Europe still demanded headlines in the Sydney papers but the people of Kurrajong were hopeful that it would soon end.

She forced a smile during the good-byes. Her mother's friends clustered around her.

"What an adventure."

"Who will manage the switchboard?"

 "You're leaving us?"

"Do write."

She clasped their hands and savored their good wishes before turning for home.

A green utility truck sat at the curb outside her front gate, the back piled with chaff bags. The handle of a pitchfork poked from among them. It was Ida Kettering, waiting, a bright green scarf knotted under her chin, her hands slipped into the pockets of her work pants.

"I need to talk with you, Rachel." She was tall, with broad bony shoulders, strong, as though these years of working on the farm had worn away what her body didn't need.

Rachel drew off her gloves. Her suitcases stood in the narrow hallway, furniture covered against the dust, her mother's organ secured in its blanket, the rugs rolled up along the baseboard. "The house is not fit to invite you in," Rachel said. "I'm leaving on the evening train."

"I've heard." Ida Kettering removed her scarf and ran her hand through her bobbed grey hair. "I'll come right to the reason I'm here. George wrote he was coming home. He's ready to take up the farm." She hesitated. "He'll be needing a wife."

Rachel's palms felt damp. "George asked after me?" She glanced up at the hawks wheeling above the gum trees. "He hasn't written me."

"George is like his daddy. Sets his mind to something but short on words to put around it." Ida Kettering drew her boot through the dirt. "This letter he sent last week, only a page, said it all." She smiled at Rachel. "I've come to tell you, he wants to set a date."

"You're asking me to marry George," Rachel studied her. "Though he hasn't formally asked?"

"He's a war hero with medals to show for it." Ida retied her scarf with a sharp twist. "You have to have faith."

"Can I see his letter?"

"It's at the farm." Ida headed for the truck.

"You didn't bring it?" Rachel called after her.

"I was in a hurry, seeing you're making plans to leave."

"How can I be sure?" Rachel asked. Not that she wanted Ida to provide an answer, just a little more time to think it through. Did George have blue eyes or brown?

"Come out to the farm, if you've a mind to. We can plan then." Ida drove off slowly, the handle of the pitchfork waving in the back, a cloud of red dust passing hazily over the latched gate. The house looked faded, abandoned already, although the wisteria vine continued to cling tenaciously to the front porch.

Rachel was tempted to toss the faded blanket aside and play her mother's organ, not those old pieces from the worn hymnal but the lilting melodies she had played as a child. She went to the kitchen and drew out the remains of a sandwich—lettuce, tomato, and the turkey she'd saved for her lunch on the train. There was time, Rachel reckoned as she leaned against the sink, for a sandwich and a hot cup of tea.

Annie's Song

They are all in the family car driving to Newcastle, to a shop her son, Colin, has discovered. A shop, he said, "with tons of instruments." He is driving. Lorna's husband, Peter, leans comfortably in the corner of the passenger seat while she sits in the back seat with her daughter, Annie.

Colin is talking to his father about the advantages of buying a fretless neck for his Fender bass guitar. "It makes an enormous difference, Dad, not having those frets." His left hand slides down through the air, fingers curled, and Lorna wonders whether he is concentrating on his driving. "The notes resonate more. You get a similar effect to the acoustic bass or the violin. You know what I mean?"

Peter knows. He played a violin years ago when he was Colin's age.

Lorna watches Annie, who is ten and excited at having her brother at home for the holidays. They don't see much of each other now he's in his final year of university. Annie's face is full of shy smiles that narrow her eyes upward, indicating her enjoyment at this adventure. She kicks her sneakers against the front seat until Lorna puts a hand on her knees to stop them. Annie is younger than her ten years, much younger. She fidgets, pulling small toys from her bag and fussing with her books. The books are all fairy tales from the Brothers Grimm, with large glossy illustrations.

"A Tab," she says. "All for myself." She hugs her favorite book to her chest. "Colin always buys me a Tab. I love my big brother," she whispers. "More even than Emily."

Emily, a gold-flecked black cat, died a year ago. She bristled with contempt for everyone except Annie. It was Emily who arrived first when Annie had her seizures.

Lorna shut her eyes against the image. Annie, three, on the kitchen floor. Colin clutching his baseball mitt to his chest.

"You've got to do something, Lorna, for God's sake!" Peter shouted. "She's not coming out of it!" Lorna called for the ambulance to take Annie to the emergency room.

"She won't die, will she?" Colin whispered.

He was protective of his little sister, confused by her disabilities. Later, when Annie came home and was asleep, Colin told Lorna he'd scared Annie so she fell off the chair.

The Mazda is noisy, used to Peter's more sedate driving. It seems to lurch between gears as Colin spins the wheel. He's talking about John Coltrane. Lorna picks up some of Annie's toys that have fallen off the seat with the motion of the car. She sees the fleshy base of Colin's neck, almost hidden by hair that needs trimming. When he was a child, the nape of his neck seemed vulnerable, a place to be protected, stroked when he buried his face in her skirt.

Over the years, Colin talked to Lorna about girlfriends and relationships, whether men are stronger than women. He wasn't wondering about physical strength when he asked. He discussed grades, roommates, and ice cream flavors. He confided shyly about his first wet dreams and asked what rape meant when she was preparing a salad for a faculty dinner party. She'd peppered the salad twice.

He likes her attention when he's trying out his latest composition, before it's quite ready for his father to hear, before he believes in it.

"Come inside and relax," he'd said. "You can't listen when you're busy like that. There's something I want you to hear."

Lorna wondered what he'd thought she'd been doing all morning, as she'd backed into him in the narrow kitchen, walked around him, stepped over his long legs while he perched on the stool at the end of the counter, his bass in his hands.

"Listen to this, Mum," he'd said. "I've written a new set of songs." They moved into the living room where his music waited on the stand. He'd opened the folder, flipped through the plastic-covered pages, and she saw how neat he had become. He had become as neat as Peter now, which surprised her. She'd sat and concentrated on this tall, mysterious son of hers, whose fingers skipped over the strings as though specially formed for just that action.

"What are the songs called?" she'd asked.

"It's a grouping of three pieces, really. I call them 'Songs for Annie.' He'd grinned at her. "You know, for the little sister."

The car rattled over the uneven road and Colin swung the wheel. Annie opened her book and turned the pages. The songs were for Annie. She'd come into their lives, when Colin was eight years old, in such fragile condition they were afraid they'd lose her. Annie, who took every bit of their energy until Lorna wanted to scream in exhaustion, sleeping in shifts through the night so they would both keep going the following day. They worried about neglecting Colin. He wove his life around theirs, adapted, and learned to wait his turn. He came to realize that only one of them could accompany him on school trips, to the ice hockey games, for pizza with his friends. He adjusted to the fragile, blanket-wrapped baby who displaced him as the central figure in the house. Her pink sleeping bags concealed the plaster cast which ran from her upper chest to her toes and kept well-meaning strangers from asking questions. There was no place for the romping, bickering, boisterous play of siblings. For two long years, there was no warm-skinned baby to hold in their arms, no tubs of bath water and soap play, no crawling under tables.

"It's a few blocks ahead," Colin says, gesturing through the windscreen. They are traveling on the outskirts of Newcastle, in the old section, where the buildings look rundown, the paint is peeling, the yards need mowing. He pulls up outside a narrow block of shops, the middle one has a window filled with guitars and amplifiers, leather straps and songbooks. The shop next door has a stained glass window; the one on the other side is boarded up.

"You want to come in with us, Mum?"

"I'll wait in the car with Annie. Don't be too long."

"My Tab?" Annie is wriggling like a puppy. "You'll get my Tab now, Colin?"

"Sure. Just snap my fingers, a Tab!" Colin presents his open hand to her. She shakes her head. He puts his hands above his head, claps them three times, twists his hand in a magician's gesture and offers an imaginary can.

"No, Colin," she giggles. "A proper Tab,"

"We'll have a Tab as soon as I show Dad this new fretless." Colin hurries into the shop with a wave of his hand.

"Songs for Annie" he'd called them. Lorna had sat on the lounge, across from her six-foot son in the battered red high-tops, his sox showing through the underside of one ripped sole. Separated from his sister by age and disability, Annie had recently become the unexpected focus of his music. He was trying to catch at something, compose a relationship.

Colin had tucked the electric bass into his chest. The melody looped down and back, flew off, centered on a phrase of notes, swung in upon itself until it was joined by a second melody and the two came together.

"You listening, Mum? Hear that? It's an alternating triplet with an eighth note there." He'd played on, looked up. "Hear the change from C# minor to F# major? You hear the difference?" He'd lifted his head. He was watching the notes imprinted in his head, his hand opened on the neck of the guitar.

While she listened she saw her children move down Chandler Road on a late September afternoon, moving away from her. Peter had just made a contraption, a trolley-board which sat on four high wheels. Annie was still confined in the full body-cast and Colin had strapped her on the trolley with dressing gown cords and was dragging her behind him. He had placed a pillow under her body against the hardness of the wood, something he had thought to do, and Laura could hear Annie's high, breathless crow as the breeze caught her fine hair and made it stand like a cock's comb. Colin was singing to her, snippets of nursery rhymes and the "Alphabet Song" from Sesame Street.

"What do you think, Mum?" The melody had come again, haunting and full, as though the notes had taken flight. She had needed to listen carefully, needed to hear the intricacies of the piece, those important supporting notes that filled the underside of the melody. As the song came to an end the notes settled high in the air, held for a heartbeat while Colin's hand hung over the instrument, then fell, dropped into her as her body reached out to receive them.

Annie is beginning to fret in the confined space of the car. "I want them to come now," she says. "I want Colin to bring me a Tab!"

"He'll be back soon," Lorna pats Annie's knees. She takes the book of fairy tales from the bag and opens it to "The Six Swans." Annie moves under her arm and turns the pages, searching for her favorite picture, the one of the young princess throwing the knitted shirts over the backs of the beautiful swans. They are changing back into human form: strapping young men except for the youngest brother. The last shirt is incomplete so he flaps one feathered arm. Annie runs her finger over the picture and stops.

"The princess made a shirt for her big brother first?" she asks the question every time they read the story.

"Yes," Lorna answers.

"This one is sick?" she asks, her finger tapped the gleaming white feathers.

"Not sick, just a little different," Lorna replies. "The princess didn't get to finish all the coats."

"He won't be able to fly, will he?" Annie said.

How should she answer? He'll learn to walk fast. He'll grow a new arm? His brothers will wait for him.

"He'll learn to manage with one arm," Lorna said.

"She should have tried harder," Annie replied. She looked out the car window. "Where is Colin? Where's my Tab?"

Jake's All Night Open

Charlotte stared past the yellow car on the hydraulic lift to the huge black bear standing against the far wall. A red blanket was tossed over one outstretched paw, a Standard Oil cap hung off its left ear. It was so lifelike she expected it to walk forward and shake her hand. An American black bear, stuffed and preserved, out here in the Australian countryside was bizarre.

The mechanic brushed her arm. "Shouldn't take long," he said. Tall and rangy, mid-twenties maybe, with freckles specked over his nose and cheekbones, he pressed a button on the wall near the bear's rump, and the yellow car slowly descended. "I'll get this baby down, yours up," he called over the hum of the machine. He leaned against the bear's side and dangled her key chain so the oversized plastic snowflake winked.

When she was ten, her father had kept a small scruffy pony named Poppet in the sunroom. All summer she had watched her father clean up its mess and replace its bed of hay. When her mother said, "I want the sunroom back. Poppet has to go." Her father leant his head against the pony's rump and cried.

Other than the bear, Jake's All Night seemed like an ordinary garage.

"You can wait in here," the mechanic called to her. She stepped around some patches of oil and stood awkwardly under the lights.

Other stuffed animals lined the wall: the head of a fox, reddish fur grey with dust; a cockatoo with all its plumage; a bull's head with a ring still in its nose; and several small heads in the corner she couldn't name. She wasn't convinced that this young mechanic could fix her car, but what choice did she have? Her car breaking down was unexpected, and the unexpected always made her nervous.

"You like Esmeralda?" he asked. His voice was muffled as he pulled off his T-shirt and hung it on the bear's nose.

"Esmeralda?" She glanced from the glassy yellow eyes to the mechanic's bare chest. *A bear called Esmeralda?*

"She belongs to Jake," he said. "Once you get used to her, she's good company. Jake says there's no other garage he knows that's got character like this one."

Jake was like her father. Her father had hidden chickens in a wire cage behind the hedge of hydrangeas, kept a goat in the tool shed, three carpet snakes slept in a tea-chest in the basement. The neighbors complained, he'd been fined, but there was always another animal to replace the ones confiscated by the police.

"You want a coke?" The mechanic pulled back the tarpaulin tacked to the wall revealing a lit-up, brightly red coke machine. "You've gotta put some money in if you want one." He kicked the machine and a can rattled into the tray. "They're cold, beautiful cold." He wiped his mouth on the back of his hand.

Charlotte wasn't sure she wanted to cross the garage. She liked the yellow car between them. "Maybe I'll take one for the trip home," she said. The sudden thought of opening her bag and exposing her wallet made her uneasy.

He put the empty coke can on top of the machine, reached up to the board behind his head for the only key hanging there. "Get this car down now, your car in." The motor of the yellow car drowned out his words.

Growing up, she'd been afraid of the pony. One day it jammed her against the sunroom wall until she nearly suffocated. "Why, Poppet wouldn't hurt a flea," her father had explained. Her mother gave the ultimatum, "Either Poppet goes, or we do." The pony disappeared and her father sulked. Her mother scrubbed the sunroom floor and opened the windows wide. It was a relief to have Poppet gone, but Charlotte felt guilty about her father's grief.

"Hey, there!" The mechanic stood at the garage door. "Can you steer this baby inside?" He tossed her the snowflake

She caught the keys clumsily. Somewhere a dog barked. Before the car door closed on her she heard the neon sign buzzing. She steered the Mazda onto the hydraulic lift while he motioned her forward.

"Right!" he called. "Beautiful!" When he opened the door of her car, she wasn't convinced by his politeness.

"I should have been in Buxton hours ago." She checked her watch.

He leaned into the engine, shook his head. He walked back to the bear and pressed the button by its rump. The Mazda rose in the air. When he looked into the car's underbelly all she saw were his sneakers tied with green luminescent laces.

"You want some music?" he called. "There," he pointed. "Over on the shelf."

Underneath the fox's head was a wooden shelf with a battered pink plastic radio. Music might be good, she thought, it would blur the soft rustles, the chinks of metal on metal. She turned the knob and the noise was deafening until she found the volume dial.

A gravelly voice was singing Mac the Knife.

"...pretty teeth, dear, and he shows them
pearly white, just a jackknife has....
keeps it out of sight..."

Sure, and she was here, on a deserted road at nine o'clock on a Friday night with a broken-down car and a mechanic she didn't trust. All this bother for an audit in Balmoral that should have been finished by midday and had her home by six.

There was a sudden *thump* under the car.

"What?" she started.

"You worried or something?" He came from under the car and looked at her. His cap had fallen off and his hair was yellow as butter. "Okay," he said. "I need to see in that engine again." The Mazda sank back down to the floor.

"It's awfully hot in here." She glanced at the coke machine. She should take off her jacket, maybe sit down. The only place was the metal stool beside the stuffed bear.

Esmeralda and Poppet. The name made the pony sound like a household pet, something benign and cuddly, housebroken and safe.

"Men are as bad as animals," her mother said as she wiped the tears from Charlotte's cheeks. "They're so unpredictable."

"You want something?" he asked.

She cleared her throat. "Everything's fine," she said. The music had stopped, and a disc jockey was gabbing about carpets, followed by the best buys to be found at Bunnies Department Store.

The mechanic grabbed his cap off the floor and pulled it on. His head disappeared into the depths of the engine. "Okay, lady, no problem." He heaved himself upright and made for the shelves on the other side of the Mazda. "You've got a blocked fuel line, is all." He grabbed his T-shirt off Esmeralda's nose and pulled it on.

She closed her eyes. He'd found the problem. She'd be leaving soon.

"*I can't give you anything but love*," he sang along with the radio. "*baaabee…*" He beat time on the shelves with his wrench, spun round and tapped lightly on the Mazda's metal hood, *bong, bong, bong,* the headlight, *ting, ting,* drummed on the rubber tire. She wanted to scream. He was wasting time. Her head felt thick and her back ached. *Tappity, tap, tap, tappity, tap, tap, tappity*—until he flipped the wrench in the air and caught it behind his back.

"You like this music?" he asked.

Now the radio was talking about homeless animals and the local shelter, that if you found a stray pet you only needed to call, night or day, they'd be there for you.

"They're waiting for me at home," she said. Why did she say *they*? She was heading home for a weekend of work. No one was waiting for her, not even a stray cat.

The mechanic held up a thin piece of tubing and squinted at it against the light. "Evenings like this one," he said, "shouldn't be cooped up in a garage with only Esmeralda for company, should be out dancing, having some fun."

Esmeralda would have been company enough for her father. He enjoyed his pets far more than he enjoyed being married. Or having a daughter.

"You ever want to just take off, catch a beat somewhere." He pretended to be dancing and dropped the piece of tubing. He knelt to pick it up then popped up like some crazy jack-in-the-box. "Yo!" He dangled the tubing in front of her face. "There's a roadhouse half a mile down the road. Doesn't close 'til two, you interested?" He was so close she could count the freckles on his nose. "We could just take off." His tone was friendly.

Before she could answer the mechanic turned and walked back to the open hood of her car. His hips were slim and his legs were long. There was a rhythm in the way he placed his feet.

She and her mother had taken off after her father was jailed. No money, no jobs, hamburger cooked a hundred different ways, and her mother trusting in horoscopes and the alignment of stars. "Life isn't about having fun," her mother explained. "You have to make choices, keep your feet on the ground." It was the summer her mother smashed all the dinner plates against the wall.

The radio was playing some sentimental melody with lots of violins, real slow-dance-music. The garage door was opened to the stars. What would it be like to just let go, forget the schedules, wear sneakers with luminescent laces? She hadn't gone dancing in years, hadn't had the time. If she was honest with herself, this was the first time she'd been invited.

"I said, 'you okay?'" He slammed the hood down. "You want to pay cash or charge?" His voice was brusque. He held up his pen.

"Charge it." She opened her purse. Somewhere people were dancing, the roadhouse lit up with couples, music and laughter.

He ran her card and she signed her name.

"You city folk work too hard." He pulled the slips of paper apart and handed her the white one. "You gotta learn to relax." He opened the Mazda's door, handed her the snowflake.

She snapped on the headlights, and Esmeralda seemed to come alive, ready to shake the foolish cap from its shaggy ear. Her hand slipped a little on the gear stick.

"Thank you." She backed out past the tow truck and the yellow car standing in the yard. The red neon sign, Jakes All Night Open, blinked out as she set the door locks tight and turned on the car radio. Big band music filled the car, another invitation to dance. Without allowing herself to think further about life's possibilities, she reached over, punched off the radio and headed off down the highway to Buxton.

Ellie

Ellie came down the footpath toward the grocery store. Two women stood gossiping on the front steps, their greyishbrown coats long to the calves of their stout legs, dark berets pulled low over their ears. They leaned close in conversation, heads bobbing, hands clutched around their dillybags. Ellie knew these women. She came on, taking small steps, little hops as she crossed the widest cracks in the pavement.

Rose Braidwood glanced around; the pompom on her beret bounced with the sudden movement, the inquisitive snap of her head. She nudged her friend, Dottie Lang. Dottie turned, stared, and drew a handkerchief from her pocket to wipe the end of her pointed nose.

"Doing the shopping for your mother, are you?" Rose said. "You're a good girl, Ellie." She swung her dilly-bag open and pulled out a scarf the color of aged pumpkin skins. "Isn't she a good girl, Dottie?"

"My, yes! A good girl." Dottie echoed. They smiled at Ellie and drew back as she mounted the steps.

"Good morning," Ellie said, mouthing the words carefully, as her mother had taught her. She was nearly seventeen and had learned these things. Then she caught the side of her coat and bobbed a short curtsey before she moved up the steps and into the shop.

She heard the women whispering behind her. Her mother had told her not to worry about whispering. Some people talk that way, her mother had explained.

Ellie came back down the footpath. In her arms she carried a bag of groceries. Her coat was too large for her and she had pushed the sleeves up from her wrists. Down the path she came, pivoting a little on her toes, past the weeping willow that flowed onto the footpath outside the Grant's yard and the lane that led to the school, by the garage that squatted at the side of the road with its huge doors open.

The smell of petrol and grease was strong, even out to the footpath. The large sign slung from the two upright posts was the only sign in the village, and so a landmark of sorts. Her face grew grave, her feet slowed as she drew abreast of the building.

She glanced at the open doorway, hefting the package to her chest so her chin rested on the rough edge of the paper. The young man was there: inside the doorway, his face was a pale oval above his dark overalls. He stood and slowly wiped the grease from his hands on an oily length of rag. His body was long and lean; his shoulders under the grey bib and straps, brown and muscled. And his hair: the shiny curls dripped onto his forehead and around his ears like the curly black hair on the Grantham's thin dog that stood behind the fence each day and growled at her as she walked to the shop.

Her tongue groped for the name of the dog, Flit. She'd heard it from her mother, who told her not to be afraid. "It would never jump the fence," her mother said. When she first passed by, she did it crab-wise, eyes fixed on the animal, until gradually the dog came to know her. Now the dog wagged its tail and whined through the netting to be petted.

Each day Ellie passed the garage, the young man came to the doorway, never into the sunlight, to watch her pass. Until today, when he stepped from the shadows.

She stopped and stood on the path with the sun on her fine hair, the package clutched as a shield against his gaze. They saw each other fully in a long look that caused Ellie to turn away.

She hurried home. She placed the groceries carefully on the back steps, and, without going inside, went to the swing that hung from the aged branch of the apple tree; a black tire tube bound by a length of rope her mother had shortened so she could swing without scraping her knees on the ground. She slid her body through the rubber tube, and with both hands taut and her back rounded to the weight, she spun and swayed, her shoes making circles in the dirt: two circles on top of one another that her mother called figures-of-eight. She leaned back and watched the mare's-tail clouds scatter across the sky. Sometimes they eddied into shapes she recognized. She tipped her head forward until her hair fell across her face, caught in the corner of her mouth. She could swing forever, until her arms tired.

Her mother called from the window. "Ellie! Did you get the things I asked?"

Ellie pointed to the front of the house. "Well, bring them in now. I'm nearly ready with lunch."

Ellie brought the bag of groceries to the table and unbuttoned her coat, letting it drop off her shoulders and slide to the floor where she stood. She pulled out a chair and sat down, her chin in her hands. "I saw some ladies," she said breathlessly. "Spoke to them." And she smiled at her mother, waiting.

Her mother glanced at her, wiped her hands on the tea towel before she swung it up to hang from the hook. "You did well, Ellie," she said. "Here's a sandwich. Mind you eat it all up this time. Stay at the table until it's finished, alright?" She looked into Ellie's eyes until the nod came. "Alright?"

That night Ellie sat at the kitchen table folding the sheets of paper, stroking each fold with her fingers so they sat flat and ready to slip into the envelopes she took one by one from the cardboard box. Every night, while her mother worked at her job, Ellie cleared the table and spread the papers out and folded them, one to an envelope, and sealed them until her tongue was sore.

"You must concentrate, Ellie. The boxes must be done each week. Some every night. Understand?" Her mother explained it all many times, showed her how to clean the table before she started, how to do each simple piece of the chore. And Ellie worked in the evenings with the radio on until her mother returned. The ones she didn't do, her mother finished the next day.

Sometimes, as she worked, Ellie remembered the city they had left, the noise and the car fumes, the rattle of trams day and night trundling by their apartment. She thought of the staircase that smelled like the inside of old shoes and zigzagged three flights past closed doors that frightened her until she came to her own.

The only green place was a small park two blocks away, with a pond hidden in a pocket of shrubs, where she sat and watched fish shadows slide through the rushes and by the rocks. The bad dreams were fading. She forgot the face of the man who drew her aside to see the flowers at the farthest end of the park. She remembered, as if in a dream, the force of his body and the hard ground, his hand beneath her dress.

His words made no sense to her, nor did his actions.

And the pile of papers grew on the table. Tonight she was doing well; she would finish them all and her mother would say what a clever girl she was to work so hard. The side of her thumb reddened from creasing the pages square and her feet tapped in time to the music on the radio.

A series of raps came at the door. At first, she mistook the sound for moths' bodies beating on the windowpane and she ignored them. When the knocking came again she realized it was someone come to call, an unusual event so late at night.

She crossed the room and opened the door. The young man from the garage stood there, leaning against the door frame, the collar of his jacket high around his neck.

The shadows made his cheekbones ridged and white, and it was those she saw first, where the skin stretched smoothly and the tiny freckles showed like the ones on early spring apples from the old tree in the yard. She stepped back, puzzled and anxious, as he moved into the room. They stood without speaking, taking measure of each other, so close she saw the fine down on his chin.

Ellie cleared a small space at the table, pushing the sheets of paper into a cluttered pile, feeling a heat in her face she had never known before. She would make a cup of tea and they would sit like her mother sat with friends, at the table, under the light.

The young man sat down carefully on a chair, his knees together, and accepted tea in the blue-onion cup. He stayed quietly there, glancing occasionally at her from downcast eyes, his hand creeping from his lap to take the teacup delicately in his fingers.

Ellie could not remember when last a man sat at their table. She wished her mother was there, and then was glad they were alone. After their tea, and as he sat on, she became restless. She wandered aimlessly round the room, unsettled by this happening, her feet rustling on the carpet square, tapping on the bare boards.

He sat so still that sometimes she almost forgot he was there. Her mind was silenced by the rush of thoughts that jostled each other, her lips unable to shape words to explain them. Until he left, leaving as silently as he had come.

The next day Ellie and her mother had breakfast together.

"The man came," said Ellie in a serious voice, a faraway look in her eyes, and a piece of toast fell to the floor.

"It's alright," her mother said. "Soon it will go away. There's nothing to be afraid of." She gathered up the toast from the floor and brushed her daughter's hair with her hand. "They are dreams, and before long there are other dreams. The old ones are gone." She collected the dishes with a clatter and began washing them in the sink.

"What will you do today?" she asked Ellie without turning, scouring the several plates over and over, sloshing the water down the cupboard doors. "Where will you go?"

Ellie had seen the leaves some days before, lustrous in the light that broke through the crowded trees. They were held in a pocket between the curve of roots; orange toadstools and moss had grown alongside in the damp soil.

The leaves were alive in some way. They pleased her, made her think of the tiny flying squirrel she had seen in the autumn, gliding from the limb overhead to a branch on an adjoining tree. She swept the leaves into her skirt, bunching it into a trough to hold the parchment-thin pieces. When the leaves were gathered, there were no fat witchity grubs left curled in the earth, just the rustle of slater beetles as they scattered under her hands.

When she returned to the house, she took down her favorite plate, and arranged the leaves at its edge, piling them with abandon until the basket of her skirt was emptied. They crackled as she patted them into order, retrieving the ones that fell to the floor, poking and settling them in a wreath shape. They were lifeless without the sunlight so she carried the plate to the table, under the lamp.

She went back to the cupboard and rummaged for the stub of candle she had saved, wiping it on her dress, straightening the black wick until it stood upright. She placed the candle in the depression at the center of the leaves, then stood back and smiled at what she had made.

That night he came, as she knew he would. She was calm this time, sitting across from him at the table with the blue onion cups. She pushed the plate with the leaves and candle toward him until it rested beside his cup, his hand.

He reached into his pocket and pulled out a wooden box, struck one of the blue-tipped matches so it flared redly and he lit the candle. She sank down in her chair and watched the flame flicker over the leaves. Flecks of orange and fawn shone, and the stems cast a lattice of shadows.

He folded the papers and she joined him in sealing them. The candle burned out as they worked and they sat on by the light of the lamp. He told her about the things he knew, and she made sense of the slowness of his words. He described the woods where she gathered the leaves, how he knew the trails, the special places where animals came. Of the fox who came through the dew-covered brush for his father's chickens. Where he set a noose for the wallaby one evening, and found it next day, with the wire caught tight in its flesh. How he shot the birds through their silver eyes with a home-made catapult when they pecked the ripening figs, and later, the fleet-winged hawks with his .22.

Ellie listened. She trusted this young man with the quiet hands. So she talked about her days, about the maidenhair fern that spilled from the moist rock crevasses at the creek and her taming of the Grantham's black dog, of the city with the dark stairs spiraling upward and the fish pond hidden in its screen of trees.

And while she talked on, he patiently folded the paper sheets into their narrow white envelopes.

Trusting Games

One day, I lost my balance while walking on a busy sidewalk in the city. Someone nearby released a sharp breath, a surprised "Oh!" Catch me, I tried to say as my body toppled toward the pavement, please catch me. A hand brushed my hair, but the gesture came too late to save me. They were frozen, panicked by the sight of an adult falling on a sunny day for no apparent reason. The moment passed. They pulled me up, stood me on my feet, brushed off my skirt and torn sleeve. Someone took my hands and flicked away the embedded gravel. They murmured condolences, gave fumbled apologies with uneasy smiles.

Daniel, my lover at the time, pushed me to ask questions, searched with me for answers, rubbed my forehead with lemon balm when the headaches became intense. How faithful he was in those early hopeful days when we both expected a diagnosis, a course of treatment, a cure. He suggested acupuncture, swimming, herbs, boiled apricot seeds. I embraced his suggestions, went from hope to hope, intent on finding answers to my illness. Nothing worked, and Daniel left me. My few friends also drifted away, and I found it a relief to be free of their questions, their well-intentioned pity.

My time now is spent with technicians and their endless opinions, technicians who think I imagine it—have let the muscles on the right side of my face contract, allowed the corner of my mouth to droop. The technicians overlook my sagging right eye; they disregard the lack of eyelashes on the upper lid. A trick, they assume—clever, but not real. So they think I pull those lashes out at night when the world sleeps, and press them under my pillow like baby teeth? They have discovered what it is not,

and for that they congratulate themselves. Their technology finds no reason
for the biting pain in my head, inside and above the right ear in the area of
the temple, and I have learned to place my right hand flat against the skin
and press for some relief.

Years ago, when I was teaching nine- and ten-year-olds, a group from
Outward Bound came to the playground to lead us all in trusting games.
In one of those games, a youngster stood on a brick wall while the others
formed two lines in front of him; they linked hands, standing shoulder to
shoulder. They made a bed with their hands, holding each other's wrists, and
the child on the wall was coaxed to turn his back and fall into those hands.
One after another the children fell. They trusted those hands to hold steady,
and once each landed, before they slipped to the ground, they rested in
their classmates' arms.

As the teacher, I was asked to do the exercise, too. All those children
with their slight wrists and small hands; some liked me, some did not. I
stood on the wall above them and saw their eager laughing faces watching
me. "Come on," some giggled. "Come on, teacher, fall!"

I was to trust these children whose faults I knew as intimately as their
handwriting? There was Jason, who stole my pencil and lied when he was
confronted in spelling class. Marion, who wrote those nasty words on the
corner of the blackboard beside my history dates. Carrie, who lost the ball,
the only ball we had for recess games. They plead. Young Tom had tears run
down his cheeks and I ignored him; he could cry at anything. This is not real,
I thought, this is not the real world below me. I listened as they gave the
countdown, 3, 2, 1. In that fraction of time I knew how a tree might fall, all
along its length. I fell and the children's hands listed, then stayed firm. They
laughed at my heaviness and said it would be easier to catch one of their
friends. "Easier," they giggled, "If we'd let you fall!"

My eyes confuse me. Double vision! Driving my car to the supermarket,
I see four blurred cars coming toward me along the yellow line. I swing
sharply on to the footpath to escape and hear only two cars pass by.

This new symptom causes a flurry of activity, dare I say, excitement. The machines roll in along with senior technicians in their starched white coats, stethoscopes readied. Their antiseptic fingers prod and stroke the side of my face, lift my eyelids. Again they fail to identify the cause, but they are anxious. Double vision means more to them than it does to me. "Come again. We have more tests," they say.

During the next invasive tests an inquisitive doctor probes with sterilized instruments beyond the back of my throat, and in the diverse and secretive canals of my lower brain finds a tumor, a rare tumor. And yet, not a tumor—cancerous cells. "Trust me," he says, "It could not be found before because it is an extra-ordinary malignancy." Everyone nods above my head, pleased with the discovery. They recognize the pain now; it has a label. I wonder at the power of names: a series of letters strung together with a unique meaning and once pronounced can be instantly understood. Fools! I hold my head carefully in the cup of my hand and wish them all to hell.

I begin the treatments. A block of days is mapped out and I survive the nausea, the time when my head flies off my neck and hangs over the sofa staring down at me. I don't know my chances. Eighteen months gives even a slow growing tumor time enough. The pain will diminish, they say, the double vision will vanish. They can't predict when my eyelashes will grow back or the muscles in my cheek tighten. My salivary glands cease to function, burned up, irradiated out of existence, and my mouth is so dry I carry a flask of cold water to water my tongue, to make speech. Practice has softened the flesh of my palm, fashioned it to fit the shape of my skull where the head narrows. I have learned to lean on the back of the chair, along the edge of the sofa, with my elbow sharply wedged into the fabric, a rigid brace for my head and its pounding.

I visit the hospital every day, same time, late morning. Everything is late these days. The hospital has a basement room with dim lighting where our pale faces present a ghostly parody of the nurses' chirpy, rosy ones. Along one wall is a bright tank with swarms of iridescent fish. A line of glittering bubbles rise continuously to the surface. Each day I come through the door,

I see those lively bubbles and they sustain me. As we wait to be called, we sit on the edges of the room, stiff and awkward, grateful for the few inches between our chairs that keep our knees from touching. No one sits on the sofa by the door. And though I stare at the sofa each morning as I wait, I can never recall its color once I leave.

This week a Smithsonian magazine lay on the table top, the swelling bud of a rhododendron on its cover. The bud is lush, mounted in white-tipped sepals, obscenely ripe—the leaves support the bud as my hand supports my pain. Today, the last day of burning, I slip the magazine into my bag. I will tack the cover on the wall across from my sofa in its blue and white cotton fabric and each day contemplate its simple promise.

The pain continues, an ever-present companion, more attentive than Daniel ever was, more faithful than any husband could be. I sleep fitfully. Sometimes the pain recedes and I breathe slowly, mindfully, only to have it return bloated with power. I plead, beg it to go away. I even barter with it. "Go away," I say, "and I'll work in Hospice for the rest of my life, I'll tithe everything for the poor, work with handicapped teenagers in their sheltered workshop." It takes no notice. "Be gentle," I whisper as a last resort, "Be gentle, pain." I fashion a pillow-trough for my head, slip three pink pills between my lips with a draft of water, and give myself up to dream.

It is the usual scenario. I am perched on the edge of a narrow brick wall. The children stand in two parallel rows as they did that sunny afternoon, years ago. This time the paved yard of the school has been replaced by gardens, great flowering gardens stretching as far as the eye can see. Rhododendrons! The children are cheering me on. "Let go," they shriek. "Let go!"

Who do they imagine stands on this wall? That younger woman who leapt at new experiences no longer lives. I don't trust a single one of them. I study them from my great height and watch as they join hands to form a latticed bed, their wrists as thin as ever. I am not going to fall!

Let go! Their cries blow up to me. *Trust us! We will catch you!* Their young faces look so appealing. Beneath the children's hands, I see a voluminous quilt of rhododendron flowers: the buds have opened and the scent is overpowering. I face the children, square my feet with the wall's rim and drop from the safety of those solid bricks, from the grip of my sleeping companion, and fall toward the fragile trellis of the children's hands.

This last barbaric course of treatments takes six weeks. There are small improvements. The double vision has gone; the dosage of cortisone and pain killers has been reduced. In our last days together Daniel wanted me to withdraw, to go to bed with the door closed and the blinds lowered. I considered his plan. The pain was unbearable at times so it seemed reasonable to give up, to attempt escape for a few days, but I was afraid that if I wrapped myself in our comforter it would become a shroud. Daniel's nerve failed, or his imagination. He couldn't distinguish between my pain and me. "I'll always care," he said as he carried his suitcase to the door and I marveled at his charity. I could understand Daniel giving up, but I had a life to live.

These days, I search my closet for head scarves to coordinate with my clothes. Under the scarf, near my ears, I insert two artificial curls that the hairdresser pressed upon me. They are soft on my skin like new-grown petals. "Trust me," the hairdresser said, "they will make you feel better." The wire twists that secure the curls are cold against my skin. My friends are surprised by the curls, for my natural hair was darker and I watch their eyes follow the contours of my scarf searching for further evidence of new-grown hair. Family members dare to smile now when I pull on a sweater and meet them for a quick lunch downtown. They smile as I take a clear soup and a small serving of quiche. Everyone pays for me, and for that, I reward them with my courage. They are grateful. A rare and exotic hothouse plant would receive less care than I do now. And every day I see the rhododendron bud tacked on my wall that will never unfold, never shrivel, never die. I begin to trust in the impossible—an everlasting bud.

Part Two

"*The witchery of living
is my whole conversation.*"

Mary Oliver
from *To Begin with, the Sweet Grass*

Monkey-eyes

Down the road he comes, a sugar bag strung on his shoulders, the rough burlap sanding his bones and his tools on his spine. Tall and lean like an underfed dingo, his father's pants rolled up his legs slapping *thwack* as he walks. It's his second day on the job.

The workmen watch him at noon-break, their eyes shaded by the jut of their caps, while he sits with his crusts dripping jam, sits apart. He squats on his heels with his head hanging down; the juice of an apple gleams wet on his chin. An apple he picked off Fergussen's tree as he rounded the split-railing fence, coming to work he reached up, not missing a step, and *snap!* swift as swatting a fly, to his pocket.

He hears the murmur of the men as they banter, the *chink* of their thermos flasks, the rustle of sandwiches unfolding in paper. The work whistle blasts, so he hitches himself to his feet, trails the men and their laughter inside the shell of the building.

In his breast pocket the picture lies snug; the glossy folds crackle when he presses his hand to his shirt. A Harley Davidson! Black and glistening, light glancing off the curves of the fender, its chrome bright as glass. He will have a motorcycle like this for his own. Like his friend, Monkey-eyes.

Monkey-eyes first appeared when he was at school, came to his shoulder and stayed through the long dragging days. Gentle friend, with the stitched button eyes, breath soft as smoke. They'd consider together the steps coming close, the teacher's pants brushing the desks, boots loud on the floor. Then, "You crazy boy! *Thwack!* You going to do it! *Thwack!* Don't look at me like that!" His desk so marked up paper rucks in the grooves as he prints, and the stains on the blotting paper blur into men and their sour-smelling mouths. The iron bars holding the desk to the floor imprison his body; he stretches his legs, slides his boots past the girl with dishwater braids, and *thwack!* again.

One day he forgets and blurts out in the schoolyard, "Monkey-eyes says these games are dumb!"

The boys look at him like he's grown two heads. They cluster and mutter, their slitted eyes wary, until the big one, Ben, draws close and yells, "Monkey-eyes! Where?" with a sneer, shoves him here and then there, chest and shoulders, and their voices come to him from a distance, sprawled out on the ground. His button-eyed, Monkey-eyes disappeared in that moment, vanished as a shadow does when you pass round a corner, but a new friend arrived, rode into the fight. This time he appeared on his motorcycle, big and powerful—came out of the voices, the pushing and screaming. The new Monkey-eyes—grinning, eyes glowing red, with the roar of his Harley and the boy, crouched, with fists thick by his face feels his friend's crazy power and swings, feels the scrape of skin upon skin, stands big Ben on his heels, flings those kids in the dust.

But the boy has learned. He doesn't let on where the crazyman waits with his black Harley gunning.

The afternoon sun drives down through the frame of the half-finished house, phantom beams cast on the boards. The crew shout to each other. A jobber yells for him to hoist up a plank, the end swings, cracks his jaw, and he closes his mouth in a scream. That's when Monkey-eyes arrives again. Comes and circles around in the disheveled yard, and he's there for the boy squinting past the studs and the pain. His crazyman, knuckles bone-white on the throttle and a mouth skewed in a high whining clamor, unsafe like the swarming of bees. The boy sees in those eyes, monkey eyes of his friend on his lush vinyl seat, that he's got to be careful. The crazyman's coming for him, comes down the center of the skeleton structure where the beams cross and lean—on his motorcycle, and in the stale air the blast of exhaust fumes are blue and the rubbery squeals warn.

This time Monkey-eyes scares him. The boy thinks to jump, swing himself to the roof beams, but he hedges. His hands are sweaty, might slip, and his legs could be snagged on the bike. The boy chooses to run, so he lunges away and reels into the yard, where he crouches low, breathing hard by a wall of stacked timber. He's safe there, while old Monkey-eyes stripes through the clefts in the walls, down the gash of the hallway, on the boards to the gravel, and into the brush.

The men stare at him from under their caps. "Aw, come on cobber," they shout. "Let it be. Ain't nothing after you!" With eyes cast down they go back to work. The boy starts to his job. His hand shakes, a tremor that rattles the hammer and misses the nail, slides off into space.

Big Sol appears, towers above with his cap pushing grey curls on his brow. "Can't go on, boy, crazy like this! Pack up!" A slap of his hand on the beam.

And he's down the road again.

He will have his own motorcycle, with money enough for a fur-covered seat and streamers that fly from the bars. He'll ride off with his friend, ride off from this dusty mean town, past Wilson's garage where Joe stands in the smell of stripped metal bodies. He'll swoop along Main Street, wipe out Grantham's mutt if he dares fly at him—paste greasy brown fur all over the road with a *Brrrrm* of his engine. The road will lie straight in front of his wheels. He won't ever look back.

Weeks go by. He's going home past Lepke's porch where the ferrets run over and down inside their wire netting cage, claws clicking like stones in a hand, teeth sharp as pins, when he meets old lady Henderson. She looks at him like she'd look at a fawning dog. "You come, and I'll find you some work," she says, pinching her mouth and stroking her hips. "There's a good days' work, if you come."

He shrugs. Sure he'll come. Do her backyard, do her! He'll sit under the boxtree with a lunch she's brought out for him in a crisp paper bag. Sure he'll come. He says, "Saturday. Early."

He works and she checks through the wrinkle of curtains. She checks for she's paying him. There's no man around to tell her if she's seeing right. A man would know by the slouch of his back, no blood is worked up, there's no sweat on his spine. She's an easy mark this Henderson lady! Taken in by his whistling, the clank of his tools.

One night he comes down the road, about dusk, when the birds are calling and the purple light strikes the paper-white gums. He knocks on her door. She comes twittering like some lonesome old starling with her cardigan pressed to protect her old breasts, and he pushes into the lighted hallway until she backs up. He is in! He smiles at the ease like an owl gliding down and in though her defenses.

She natters on, with her back to the wall, about Saturday next, and the work still to do, the leaves falling fast. Her lips move like two soft worms. Her breath is fast and choked and smelling of onions from a stew, he can tell. He is hungry. He sees all the gimcracks, the lamps with pale shades all alight and the lounge looking clean.

He stands in her hall gazing through, not moving at all, so she hovers, her tongue clattering on. He ignores the string of her sentences, watches past the top of her head, until he's ready, and then he stares her full in the face. She skids to a halt, her mouth sags, drops open like she's been hit. Like his mother's mouth, loose and red.

Sure, he'll come again. Next Saturday, *thank you, thank you!* He turns and she moves this way and that, weighing will she squeeze past him to unlock the door. But the hall is too narrow, and he makes himself broad; his shadow falls up and over the door, and he likes that. He follows his size with admiring eyes as she dithers behind him. What's the hurry, he wants to ask, when my shadow is big? The wall is dwarfed? He moves then to open the door, and his hand is steady. He opens it slowly.

Up the road a magical mopoke cries. It cries and the echo comes back from its mate, cries again and the night is down.

He had money once, but come Mother's Day, he spent it on blue fluffy slippers. His father moved fast on the balls of his feet, his eyes shot with blood, his face flushed. "Don't know who you are, boy! Some crazy boy to spend all your money on these!" And his father throws the box at the wall, sends the blue slippers flying, the bright mirror smashing. The white tissue paper floats past his mother who stands with her face puckered up and her hair frizzed like a golliwog's.

"You crazy boy!" his father shouts again. The boy ducks clear of his father's fist and wine-sodden breath, races out to the door on the stray chips of mirror to his friend who sits easy on the smart vinyl seat. "We can go!" the boy says.

"Gotta get me a bike," he mutters. Then loud to the stars, "Gotta get me a bike!" The crazyman sways on the shiny black seat and moans with approval; his one seeing eye glints green as the rags on his back, and he wheels the bike forward alongside the boy, glides over the ruts with whistling wheels. The boy knows the machine as it moves under him, smooth as hours slipping by, and his fingers caress the chrome, feels the rag in his hand as he polishes. His bike! Old tight-fisted Henderson has money, he confides to his friend on the road, by the look of her house and her lamps, by her clothes. *Yes, yes!* they agree. He can smell the leather of his steel-toed boots, knows the power in the silver exhausts. They will visit her one night, but carefully, carefully!

A torn moon and a night full of whispers; he steps on the road that humps to the patches of sand, marked where the wombats have gone to the creek, the frog's shouting. He comes with the monkey-eyed man sidling up, the tang of gasoline for company.

The house is dark. The chair on the porch has whale ribs blanched in the light throwing shadows that break on the walls; the window is square and fine-screened. He takes the chair with a stealth that silences his boots to the window, peers in to the looming white fridge and the countertop streaked with his shape. He unfastens the screen with a twist of his wrist at each latch and the puny clips snap like the back of a mouse underfoot. He props the frame on the chair, slides up the pane with a nod of relief to his friend. Monkey-eyes brings his bike to the side of the steps like a bat, dark and cave-smelling.

The boy stops. His hand freezes over the objects outlined on the sill. Small shapes, two inches apart, standing colored in the moon's light, each one in its own perfect place. Jugs! Tiny spouts and curved handles, blue, pink, green, brown. The one under his wrist has a small spray of flowers, three roses or such leaning out of its lip. His foot may have kicked, might have smashed, sent those jugs flying, an alarm in the dead of the job. So he carefully lifts each one to the counter and his fingers move blindly like sweet worms in the earth until the window is cleared for his boots.

He pulls himself in with a flick of his back, his legs doubled up in the square, holds his breath, and the torch at his belt grinds into the bulge growing large in the crotch of his pants. Old Monkey-eyes skims up the few stairs to the porch and sets his feet on the Harley's handlebars. *Let's go!* Shaped by the twist of his mouth, *let's goooooo!*

The boy is gone, his feet touch the floor, smooth and swept like a sheet of glass or unbroken mirror. There's a shaft of light in the dark, for the curtains are parted, and his eyes adjust like an owl's seeking prey. A choked snore rises from the room at his left where the door is open, and he moves there. He watches the eiderdown rounding the body, stretched taut from the foot of the bed to the nose that hooks, ridged at the top. One of her arms is flung out on the pillow, an old stringy arm that curves round her head where her eyes are sunk in the hood of her brows. The snore comes again. She must be dreaming, he thinks, of young boys on their knees, sweeping leaves, raking gravel at her bidding. *Yes, ma'am, no ma'am!*

Her bag is on the chair by the lamp, its handle looped in a noose as it hangs off the seat, a fat leather bag with its clasp shining gold. He opens it up, grabs the wallet, spills a lipstick, a comb, and a shower of papers hit the carpet. In the wallet he finds a bundle of notes, neatly folded, and a cascade of coins chink into his pocket, like snatching apples. *Sweet and sweet!*

I've got me a bike! running round in his head like a drum beat. Then the snore comes again, fractured, caught in her throat, and the covers slide round till her pale wrinkled neck is exposed. Is there! He remembers he snapped the grey ferret's neck with a jerk of his thumbs and the blood running down on the teeth that had bitten him. If she wakes, then he'll show her! The eiderdown settles with a grunt, and the night has a powdery smell.

To the window, onto the chair with a thud of his boots, and the crazyman howls, slings his feet from the handlebars, accelerates slow with a *vroom!* that is music. The boy replaces the jugs one by one, sets them carefully down on the sill, breaks a rose, spreads the petals for a signal he's been like a dog leaves his scent when he's proud.

His crazyman's waiting; now they can go! The boy strides down the steps and onto the road. "I've got me a bike—this is it!" The flimsy cash flaps in his hand. "I'm coming!" he shouts to the pale-pointed stars, and Monkey-eyes crows with delight, rips up through the gears, and pops his front wheel, a salute. He'll never look back up the path to his door, won't look back at the draggle of gardens, those dead hollyhocks standing like toothpicks. He won't think of the people who sleep there, iron beds creaking. He'll ride out of the town with a high-flying thumb, with Monkey-eyes close like a shadow, past the gates barred against him, the apples that fit in his palm.

Rhubard Pie

"Get out of my garden!" Sadie came down the steps, letting her heels ring, gun level in her hands. "Mulligan!" She yelled. "You don't listen. Just like Mel Tomkins when I tell him to keep you leashed up."

The dog leaned into the rhubarb plant and eyed her. It yawned with its jaws wide open, lost its balance and sprawled among the rhubarb leaves. The stalks popped and snapped like firecrackers.

"Get out of my rhubarb!" Sadie yelled again.

The dog slunk away to the fence, tail curled into its back legs. "Mel should know better," she muttered. "No sense at all taking up with that city woman." Sadie's eyes narrowed. "Sniffing around like a bitch in heat, looking for more than the job in hand. She's no better'n the animals she fills her barn with." Sadie noticed how thin Mulligan had become, how the bones stood out on his hind quarters. She knew what the city woman had done to the Lumley place, making it look like something out of a slick magazine, not a place you'd want to live in anymore.

The dog turned and came a few tentative steps into the yard, snout lowered. "You stay away!" she called as she raised the gun to her shoulder. She wasn't about to have him in her garden again.

Sadie left the body of the dog beside the fence while she gathered up the trampled rhubarb stalks. "What a mess you've made, Mulligan," she muttered as she spread loose dirt over the blood spatters and propped up the splayed parsley plants. She wrapped Mulligan in an old blanket and tied the twine over and round the bundle as though it were a slab of beef. The blanket dipped and hooped on the bend of the legs, the curve of the head. "Didn't like you much, dog, and that's the truth. What I think to tell him when he comes looking for you will have to wait."

The dog's weight settled in her arms as she pushed the kitchen door open with her boot, and tipped it down on the floor by the side of the stove. She propped the gun against the wall near the blanket. "Think he can work for me one day, her the next. We'll see about that." She selected a length of wood from the stack by the wall and shoved it into the firebox. "Think with money she can have anything she wants out here."

Sadie washed her hands at the sink, pulled an apron over her head. She placed everything out on the table—rhubarb stalks, flour, butter and eggs, milk and bowl. "This pie, now, will take my mind off you. And him for a while."

She made the dough, rolling it out so the wooden pin traced large M's on the floury dough, clicking rhythmically against the signet ring she wore, the ring her father had left for her, along with the farm, when he died. She glanced at the lump of blanket. "Shouldn't have come back down, all the warnings I've given, shouldn't have dared." The pastry flattened, shaped roundly and thin enough for a crisp crust. She laid the pastry in the bottom of the dish and ladled the rhubarb mixture on top, setting the white china bird in the center, beak raised and open for the escaping steam. "He'll be down sometime, I expect, when he finishes work." She rolled out the second round of dough and fashioned it to fit, cutting off the overhang with the knife, her fork leaving bird-marks around the edge.

As she wiped her hands on her apron, a car pulled into her driveway. Footsteps sounded on the path, followed by a series of knocks, loud and rattling on the outside screen door. Neighbors wouldn't be about at supper time unless it was an emergency. Not in any cars. She didn't hear her name called so it wasn't Mel or Frannie James from across the road. She hung her apron on the back of the chair.

Across the porch she could make out the figure of a woman standing at the foot of the steps. "What do you want?" she swung open the front door, keeping the screen latched, thinning her voice against the quiet of the evening.

"Sorry to bother you." The young woman sounded anxious. "I'm lost."

Sadie half-opened the screen door. The woman stood uneasily in the blade of light thrown through the opening. She was dressed in a smart city coat and clutched a big handbag. Her face was made up, lipstick and rouge, or maybe it was just that her cheeks were flushed. You couldn't be too careful with the world the way it was, even out here in the bush where everyone thought they knew everyone else.

"Can I use your phone?" She lifted the handbag and held it against her chest. The barking of Franny James' dog came through the trees. "I'm on my way to a friend's house and I'm lost," she paused. "I'm awfully late."

Tonight of all nights! Someone coming in off the road and wanting a phone and what should she say? The telephone lines were clear for anyone to see; she couldn't say no. "You can call," she said, opening the door a little wider.

The young woman murmured her thanks and came onto the porch. "I won't be a moment," she said. "It's very kind of you, really." She held out her hand awkwardly. "I'm Lillian Mathieson." Sadie touched her outstretched hand and pointed to the phone on the inside wall. Lillian took it down and dialed. Sadie could hear the ringing through the line.

"She might have gone up the road to look out for me," Lillian said, a breathless rush to her words. "I can't think where she could be tonight, expecting me for supper."

Sadie washed the last of the flour off her hands and wiped them on a tea towel. "Lots of things get done at night," she glanced at Mulligan to confirm he was securely tied. "Work doesn't stop out here just because it gets dark."

Lillian stood by the table pulling at the zipper on her bag, opening it a little, zipping it closed again.

"Who are you visiting?" Sadie asked.

"Joanna Freeman," she replied. "She lives out here somewhere. I seemed to drive for hours."

"Freeman?" Sadie checked the fire's heat then slipped the pie into the oven. "She bought the Lumley's old place. I know someone who works for her."

"I haven't seen her since she bought the farm," Lillian said. "I used to work for her." She paused. "She was senior to me but we were friends, good friends."

"Good friends?" Sadie asked. "Kinda hard when she's your boss?"

The girl shrugged. "Our families know each other," she looked round the room, taking in the mess of baking, the heat of the fire.

"Better sit down," Sadie said. It wouldn't hurt to have this girl stay, wouldn't hurt at all when Mel came calling, and Mulligan being missed about now. "You can try her again in a minute."

"She has horses," Lillian added.

"I've seen them." Sadie had seen the horses, smack in the middle of her alfalfa field and the fence knocked down. Two days work to rebuild and words between them hot enough to shake that woman good, make her see what you can and can't get away with out here.

"The pie smells good," Lillian unbuttoned her coat and put her bag on the floor. "It's warm in here. I didn't know wood fires could get so hot."

Sadie put her apron back on and tied the strings. "You want a cup of coffee?" she asked as she slid the kettle onto the stove. She gathered up the rhubarb leaves in newspaper, scraped the table clear of flour and leftover dough with the blunt edge of the knife.

"I should try again." Lillian looked over at the phone. Sadie wiped down the table top.

"Wood stove's best for cooking." Sadie put two mugs on the table. "Choosing the right wood takes practice."

The girl wiped the corners of her mouth with a painted fingernail. "I heard that dog barking across the street," she said. "I thought it would choke itself."

The kettle whistled and Sadie spooned instant coffee into the mugs, put three sugars in her own and stirred them both. The girl cradled the mug in her hands.

"No dogs will bother you here," Sadie said. "No loose dogs round here for miles."

"I don't like being out in the dark like this." Lillian stared at the window where the blind was pulled against the night. "Maybe you can give me directions and I can leave."

"You're not far off, other side of this hill," Sadie nodded toward the back door. "Have your coffee. No sense in rushing."

"Do you mind?" Lillian pointed at the phone again. "She's probably there now." Lillian was on her feet, hand reaching.

"Go ahead," Sadie nodded.

Lillian dialed and held the phone to her ear. The dull burring seemed loud in the quiet of the kitchen.

"Still not answering?" Sadie smiled. They'll be searching for the dog most likely, she thought, calling for him round the barn.

The girl sat down on the edge of her chair. "She wouldn't forget I was coming. We've been planning this for months. It's the roads—no signs, no streetlamps." She opened her handbag. "Do you mind if I smoke?"

Sadie put out a saucer. "Go ahead," she said. Lillian Mathieson rummaged in her bag and produced a cigarette case and silver lighter. She took a sip of coffee.

"Sadie Harris!" It was Mel shouting her name; his voice harsh like he was calling his hogs for supper.

The girl almost dropped her lit cigarette into her mug.

"You there?" The voice came from behind the house, high and urgent. "You seen Mulligan?" Sadie remembered when his voice sounded like warm syrup on newly grilled pancakes. She smoothed her apron and looked over at the blanket. "It's all right," Sadie said. "It's Mel Tompkins, from up the hill. Come to get his dog."

"Dog?" Lillian's mouth stayed open on the question.

Sadie touched the hump of blanket with her boot as she moved to open the back door. Mel Tompkins stood in the yard with his hands in his trouser pockets. He looked like he'd come in a hurry with his coat unbuttoned and hanging on his thin shoulders, his pants rolled above his boots.

"Told you to keep him away from my property. Told you to tie him up." She put her hands on her hips; they were safe on her hips. "He came one time too many, Mel."

"You've got him?" He took a step forward. "Where?"

"By the fire," she replied.

Mel relaxed. His handsome face, lit up from the kitchen light, was long and narrow and angry. "I'll take him home then. You send him out to me."

"You'll have to carry him," Sadie said.

"Carry him?" Mel wiped his mouth with the side of his hand.

Sadie folded her arms across her chest. "Like I warned you!" Mel wasn't so friendly anymore, taking up with fancy money, turning his back on folks who'd always known him, giving notice with little thanks for all she'd planned for them. Her farm not good enough, not the money for fancy changes and eating out in town like some could.

"Mulligan!" Mel called. "Here, Mulligan!" He stared at Sadie and set one foot on the bottom step, as though he might rush the stairs. "You didn't...?"

"Don't you come up those stairs," Sadie said. "I've got a visitor here." She beckoned Lillian to come to the door. The girl was sitting with her mouth slack and the cigarette burning away between her fingers. "Come on," Sadie said brusquely, "I want Mel to see you."

"I don't want to get involved," Lillian said faintly.

"You shot him?" Mel shouted at Sadie. "Shot Mulligan?"

Lillian stared at Sadie in disbelief. "You shot his dog?"

"It's there," Sadie pointed into the kitchen, "Been there all the time." She swung back to face him. "This is Lillian. She's on her way to Joanna Freeman's."

Mel took several steps toward Sadie, his hand on the railing. "Give him to me..."

The girl stood behind Sadie. "Mr. Tomkins, I don't know anything about your dog. I just got here."

"You shouldn't have done it, Sadie Harris!" He came to the top step.

"You're trespassing on my property, Mel." Sadie reached along the wall and took hold of the gun. She swung it smoothly into her shoulder and concentrated down the barrel. "That's as far as you come, Mel." Without taking her eyes off him, she said to Lillian, "Pick up the dog."

"I can't touch that thing," Lillian whispered.

"Pick it up and give it to Mel, here." Sadie's voice was firm. She didn't want to waste any more time. Her rhubarb pie was ready. She could smell its doneness. "Now!" she ordered.

Lillian pulled the bundle away from the side of the stove and started to lift it. One of the dog's forepaws poked stiffly through a fold in the blanket. "I don't believe this," she murmured.

Sadie moved aside to let Lillian pass. Mel extended his arms so Lillian could drop the bundle into them. "I'll get you for this," Mel muttered.

"She offers you a few more dollars and you think you can leave here just like that!" Sadie held the gun steady. "You stay in good with her for you'll not be working here again."

Mel Tomkins hefted the bundle high on his chest; the dog's leg brushed his cheek. When he walked across the yard and he didn't look back.

"That's the way it is, Mel," she called, "You know that!"

Sadie stood the gun back against the wall. She grabbed a towel and took the pie out of the oven; the crust was beginning to darken on the edges. Another few minutes and she'd have been too late. Lillian stood at the front door.

"Follow this road and you'll see a yellow mailbox, that's your friend's place." Sadie folded the warm towel in half and hung it over the oven rail. "They'll be there by the time you arrive."

Lillian paused, her hand on the doorknob. "Who'll be there?"

"The two of them," Sadie replied. "Mel's taken up with your friend, Freeman. He works for her, works real hard." She cut the rhubarb pie into neat triangular wedges, then ran her finger up the blade of the knife and licked the juice from its tip. "You leave now, you'll be in time to bury Mulligan."

Piggy-wig

The crib was close about his body, so close that his feet hit the end bars. "Lovey," he crooned. "Lovey." He twisted the piece of faded blanket around his fist and down his cheek, his waking time. He rolled onto his belly and slid over the handrail until his toes touched cold linoleum. Every morning he tried to hit the square with the yellow flower, a flower like the yellow ones in the garden outside the window.

He held the wall as he moved to the kitchen, his stomach uneasy. Her bedroom door was open, and he checked to see if dada had returned, but she was alone. The mound of bedclothes stirred, his mother's outstretched arm moved back under the comforter. She was alone. The new man who wore the T-shirt with an eagle on its back hadn't stayed.

Once there had been a man called dada, a grayish man who laughed a lot. He remembered the smell of his sweater like the oil he slicked on his hair. The man played a game on his toes, singing about pigs and roast beef. The song arrived in a curling wisp like the blue smoke drifting upward from dada's cigarette, *Piggy-wig, piggy-wig, funny little piggy-wig.* He felt the tweaking of his smallest toe as it cried all the way home.

One day dada was gone. All his clothes left the closet—his wooly coat, the leather boots by the back door. His mother didn't speak for the longest time. She played cards on the big table, slapping them down, shuffling them so hard the cards bent in two. She walked the dog in the afternoon and talked on the phone. One morning she said, "You've done it again, Frog," and she moved his crib from the corner of the bedroom into the storage closet.

In the kitchen the small white dog moved in its metal crate by the stove. The boy pushed away one of the dog's squeaky toys and hurried to the plastic bowl on the floor. They reached the bowl of food together. The dog growled but the child was stronger. "No, Doozie," he scolded. He scooped the lumps of chow into his mouth while the dog sat with its paws high-stepping on the floor, ready to gobble up the spilled fragments.

The closet door banged and his mother's footsteps came down the hall. She stood in the hallway, tall above him, the sleeping shirt creased to the folds of her body. "Not again! How many times do I have to tell you?" She dragged him up onto the kitchen chair, and swung the cupboard doors open and shut, put the speckled bowl on the table, shook in the cereal flakes. She pressed a spoon into his limp fingers. "Hold it!" she commanded like all the other commands. "Sit up! Close your mouth! Don't rub yourself there!" She leaned over the table, her face flush with his. "I've nearly had it!"

She glanced at the scattered toys under the window, the plastic toy box, his red tin ambulance beside the carefully balanced tower of wooden blocks. "You're not stupid, God knows." She jerked open the curtains. Birds hovered at the feeder that his dada had hung there on the tree. He remembered the names—willy-wagtail, robin redbreast, sparrow, crow.

His mother was staring at the wall where the pictures she'd cut from magazines were pinned above his reach, colorful pictures of mountains and big houses and oceans. He liked the colors but not the spidery figures made from the tree's shadows beneath them. His house could be scary. One night they'd heard bumps and shrill voices through the wall. "There you go, Frog, Harry's home again. There'll be some fun for Edie tonight."

Smoke rose from her cigarette. "You want to catch it, Frog? Look!" She stretched her fingers through the smoke making it wheel and eddy, breaking the plume, brushing it toward the ceiling. "See, it's gone, just like everything else. You think you've caught something, and presto, it's gone."

The dog had followed them to the table and was lying near her chair. "Here, Doozie!" she snapped her fingers.

"Silly Dooz," he thought as she rubbed its ears with her shoe, the dog's tail slapping the table leg.

She picked up the dog and sat it on her lap, scratching the fur beneath its jaw. He wanted to be there, held and stroked. He remembered her smell and softness before she pushed him away. "Every time you climb on me you want to suck!" she'd said, legs opening so he slipped to the floor.

She crushed the cigarette out in the saucer among the other butts and plopped the dog on the floor. "I'm going to Jill's for a while." She headed into the bedroom. "He's got a room there, but Jill wants him to move out, and if I don't let him come here, he'll be gone." The words were punctuated by drawers slamming. "That's the way it is, Frog. You have to make things happen sometimes."

The room was stuffy. He watched the cereal sink in the blue bowl, the spoon slowly fill with liquid. He'd build another tower with chimneys and masts, and he'd put his fire engine inside with the animals. If there was a fire, they'd be safe.

When she stood in the doorway the little dog strutted round her legs. Her dress was covered in large flowers with a belt and a big silver buckle. The flowers were yellow like the floor rug in his room. She put it on each time she left him.

"I'll be back soon. Can't be with you all the time, Frog, you know that." She froze, mid-thought. "I need someone to talk to." Her eyes flicked round the room. "He's going to come back tonight. And maybe he'll stay." She returned to the bedroom and came back with a suitcase. He had never seen her take a suitcase to Jill's before, all the times she'd gone. She gestured at the case. "It's all right. It's for his clothes."

She touched his head, brushed his hair back. Then she pulled a leash out of the broom closet and a plaid doggy-coat she'd bought last winter. "Here, Doozie!" Catching the dog to her, she snapped on the coat, fastened the leash. The dog whimpered excitedly in her arms. "Can't let Doozie run loose, Frog, he might get killed out there." A strip of light flashed through the kitchen before the door was closed. "You be good now, Frog." He heard the click of the lock as the key turned.

He went into her bedroom and sniffed the air. She'd forgotten to put away the bottles and jars with the purple flowers on them. He lifted a squat jar and unscrewed the lid, prying with his fingers into the milky-white cream, rubbing it over his cheeks. She'd warned him about touching anything on her dressing table. "You only waste it, Frog. It's all I have for the world out there." Usually she locked everything up in the side cupboard.

Her shirt, the one she slept in, lay on the bed. He pulled it over his head, holding his breath as he felt its softness. He raised his arms so he didn't step on the hem. In her bed, he found where the indentation of her body was set in the mattress. He stretched long between the cool sheets, his toes feeling the space. He didn't need his blanket when he was in her bed.

They came home together while he was building another tower of blocks, she and the eagle-man and Doozie on his leash. The eagle-man poked him in the chest, "Long time no see!" He patted the yellow flower on the back of his mother's dress and sat at the table. She set the Chinese food out on three plates and brought one plate to the small table where his tower stood. She handed him a spoon. He listened as they talked and laughed together. The dog skittered around the table begging for scraps.

Later that night, he made a fort out of blocks with three walls and a roof, big enough to hide the red ambulance. Then he made two walls of small blocks and lined up his dark green tanks on one side, his two helicopters on the other. He searched in his box of toys and found the plastic soldiers and arranged them in a circle with their guns facing in. He sorted through the farm animals and found the little white dog. He placed the dog in the center of the circle and bunched the cows and horses around it, all of them facing the soldiers and tanks.

The eagle-man came over to his table. "You playing war?" he asked. He marched the tanks down the table. "*Bang, bang, bang,*" and swiveled the long guns on the green tanks. He knocked the animals over, one by one, and then drove the ambulance out of the building to carry them off. He stacked the animals at the side of the tower. "Gotta keep them, Frog," he said. "Gotta have food for the army men." When the eagle-man was done flying the helicopters he went back to the sofa and the television laughter. The little white dog jumped up on his lap and licked the eagle-man's hands.

The boy cleared the table of tanks and helicopters, packed the animals in his toy box, and built another tower. When the screen went blank he knew it was time for bed. "We'll play war tomorrow, kid," the man called as he left the living room. They didn't shut the bedroom door and the sounds from the bedroom made him hold his ears.

Later, the brightness of the streetlamps woke him. He walked past the open bedroom door and into the kitchen without switching on the light. "Here, Doozie," he whispered as he unlatched the door of the crate and reached for the squeaky toy. The dog came to him and he held its collar tightly. "Bad Doozie," he said, leading the little dog toward the door. It pulled back against the boy's grip, its hind legs scrabbling on the floor.

"Come on," and he made the sucking noises dada once made when he didn't want to eat his food. The rubber toy squeaked as he reached for the doorknob. "Shush," he hissed. He yanked the dog by its collar and reached for the iron key sitting in the lock.

He opened the door just wide enough to shove the little dog out into the night. *Little piggy goes to market!* He threw the rubber toy down the steps. *Little piggy stays at home!*

"Bye, bye, Doozie," he called softly and shuffled back down the hall to his bed.

Home on the Night Train

Joey King came home from Sydney for his father's funeral. The steam from the train whipped round his legs as he stepped down to the platform and when the lights on the train pulled away everything beyond the station became very dark. Joey hitched his vinyl bag on his shoulders and buttoned his coat as he picked his way across the railway lines and through the white-washed railway gates. He hadn't thought to bring a flashlight but his feet knew the way.

Mrs. Worthy's downstairs lights were on, and he heard the muffled barking of her dog; Charlie was on lookout again. He knew he should stop and tell his sister, Patricia, he was here for the service, but he took the side road instead. He had to see the damage for himself before he spoke to anyone. The hot damp smell of burning still filled the air and when he saw what was left of their childhood home he stopped abruptly at the gate posts.

The frame of the back bedroom, with the door held closed as it always had been, stood out against the sky. The east wall remained standing, as did the fireplace chimney. The kitchen stove was crushed under a heavy blackened beam and charred debris criss-crossed the living room floor. Joey kicked some timber away and felt glass under his shoes. In the kitchen he saw the remains of the long trestle table where he and his two older brothers had sat for meals, their father with his back against the warmth of the cook stove, Patricia opposite him where their mother once sat.

Joey sat down on a slab of board, a part of the wall by the look of the faint blue stripes on the singed wallpaper. A large enamel pan lay beyond his shoes, filled with dark water, and the moon reflected in it like a giant broken egg. The chicken run used to be over there to the left beyond the wedge of blackened chimney where, now, all he could see was a tangle of scorched wire netting. They'd built the coop one year. Dan talked of it often, how he and Ricky had helped their father, cutting and sawing, nailing the great bale of wire netting round the posts. It was one memory the boys clung to as their father drew away from them.

"We ran out of nails," Dan would say sullenly.

"The posts fell over," Ricky answered, his breath wheezing in his chest. "The netting came down in a heap right on top of me." His asthma always got worse when he got excited.

"You lost the hammer," Dan accused.

"I found it, you remember, in the grass."

"Dad was putting on the roof, cursing like mad when he hit his thumb." Dan remembered the details. "We finished it though." Dan's voice lifted for a moment. "It was a beauty!"

"A real beauty!" Ricky agreed.

Dan had collected the eggs twice a day, but as he got older he passed on the job, first to Ricky, then to Joey. That's the way it was in those years, everything passed down the line from eldest to youngest, like their coats and pants, and who took over collecting eggs when he stopped? Patricia most likely and no one thought to thank her.

Joey heard the lonely two-note call of a mopoke off in the trees.

One night, as a child, he'd heard the night bird calling and cried out, not sure why he was frightened. He'd expected his mother to come but it was Patricia who came and held him, told him to go back to sleep. "It's only the night bird calling for its mate," she said.

"I want him to stop." Joey whispered. "I want the other bird to come."

Joey glanced at the frame of the bedroom door, the room their father refused to let them use. Patricia had suggested that Joey take the downstairs bedroom; the boys were getting bigger and the three of them filled the upstairs bedroom to bursting. Their clothes were tangled

together in the single closet and his brothers were beginning to care,
wanting to spruce up for the girls.

"It's where your mother died," their father had said. "No one goes in
that room again."

When Patricia protested he was adamant. "Not another word, Patty!"

He had locked the door and put the key high in the kitchen cabinet.
So the room stayed as it was—the bed covered in its floral bedspread, the
dresser topped with a dusty oval mirror, the wardrobe doors closed on
hangers still filled with their mother's clothes, her dresses and coats.

Joey knew the story—how his difficult birth had drained his mother's
strength, how she never fully recovered. "He's the one did it to your mother,"
his father had said, more than once, after his evening beers. His father
nursed their mother through the last year, large clumsy hands brushing her
hair, helping her in and out of bed, setting her meals on a tray he bought
just for her.

It was Neville's coat hanging near the bedroom door that caused
Joey's leaving. Neville was warned to stay away, but he and Patricia met
in secret at the house those nights when the darts matches were played
at the Ball and Barrel. One night, their father came home early after a
match was canceled. Patricia heard their father coming up the path,
grabbed the key from the kitchen cupboard, and pushed Neville into the
back bedroom. Their father found Neville in the bedroom, grabbed his
shirt and pushed him down the back steps. "Get out!" he yelled. "You see
Patricia in church, or not at all." He threw Neville's coat over the steps so
the arms flew wide and fell over the boy's head.

"Did you know he was here?" he asked Joey. Joey had bounded down
the stairs when he heard his father's shouting.

"Joseph has no part in it," Patricia stood between them, her face flushed.

"Don't talk back to me, Patty." He pushed Patricia aside.

"You always pick on him," she shouted. "Leave him alone." And Joey was
out the open door and into the night. "I hate you!" he heard Patricia scream
at their father. "Hate you!"

Next morning when Joey came home, he packed his vinyl bag. Patricia sat at the kitchen table with the breakfast dishes not cleared and he saw it was only his father's set of plates on the table. Patricia was dressed in the same clothes she had worn the night before.

"You okay?" he asked.

Her face was set and pale.

"I'm going," Joey said, "to Aunt Sal's." Dan and Rick had gone to their mother's sister in Sydney while they looked for jobs. He'd saved enough money from egg sales to pay for a train ticket and he'd find work, too, once he was in the city.

"It won't happen again," Patricia said softly. "Please stay."

"The others have gone," he said. "Neville will come back."

He barely recognized her sitting so quietly in his mother's chair. "I don't know if I can stand this much longer." She glanced at the cupboard where the bedroom key was kept.

"Then do something," he said. "Come to Sydney with me."

Patricia rose stiffly to open the kitchen door. She carried her right arm against her side. "It's nothing, Joey. I fell. Take care of yourself."

Joey picked his way through the mess of timbers to the bedroom door and felt the blistered paint, ran his hand over the doorknob. How had it withstood the fire? He remembered, after his mother died, climbing on a chair to reach the key and going into the room. The iron frame of the bed was now a twisted mass in the corner, but he remembered lying under its covers, and once he had crawled into the safety of his mother's closet. With the door shut it had been dark and warm and smelled of lavender.

He heard Charlie barking again.

Joey had found the sleek blue kelpie when he was coming home from school one day. The dog had been wandering along the road without a collar, thirsty and abandoned. His father had liked the dog, liked the way the kelpie leaned against his leg so his head could be stroked. "You watch out for him," he'd said to Joey.

The dog had stayed close to Joey for several weeks without disturbing anyone until one Saturday when he dug under the fence of the chicken run.

"Get rid of it, Joey!" His father had said. "Five dead hens, you need to get five more."

"Let Joseph keep the dog," Patricia had said. "It won't happen again."

"Hear me?" said their father.

So, Mrs. Worthy had given Charlie a home, just like she'd done for each of them in turn, but Charlie had stayed.

The stars were brighter here above the leveled house, brighter than they were in the city. Joey heard the rustle of small animals and the scrape of footsteps along the outside path. Mrs. Worthy had heard the train leave; she had come to find him.

"Nothing you can do here, Joseph!" she called. She used his old name like Patricia. In the city they called him Joey, but he liked Joseph; it gave him something of his childhood, and hadn't his mother named him? "You come over to the house, now; Charlie knows you're here. The bed's there for you on the verandah, some fresh bread and lamb chops." Her shoes scraped on the path. "Patricia's waiting."

"I can't come yet," Joey replied. He knew Mrs. Worthy had said her piece in the past, about their father's behavior toward them all, but she was kind to Patricia, kind to all the boys.

"It's a shock," she answered. "We did what we could." Her grey hair stood round her head like a silvery halo and she'd take that as a compliment if he told her. She held the local church together, arranged the flowers brought from her garden, had her name engraved on the front pew.

"How did it happen?" he asked.

It was clear Mrs. Worthy had been waiting for him to ask. "It was last Tuesday. Your father must have come home late. Charlie was barking like crazy so I woke up and went to look outside. You could see the fire clear between the trees. And the smoke so thick." Her voice rose as though even now she was beating back the flames. "I called the fire brigade, put on my coat, and I came."

"Patricia?"

"Your father was angry she was seeing Neville again so she was staying with me." Mrs. Worthy paused. "When I got here, she was kneeling beside him." Mrs. Worthy paused. The wind sifted through the beams. "She wasn't herself, poor lamb."

"How did the fire start?"

"Seems it started in the kitchen," Mrs. Worthy said. "Your father was getting a little forgetful." Joey hadn't seen his father in months, but he had heard from Patricia that their father was drinking more heavily, spending more time at the Ball and Barrel, playing darts late into the night.

"Can you keep supper for me? I'll come in a bit."

"Take your time, Joseph," Mrs. Worthy shuffled back up the path. "Patricia will wait up for you."

Above the east wall he saw the Southern Cross and across from its five bright stars was the Milky Way like a brushstroke of whitewash on the roughened surface of the sky. Patricia had tried to mother him. "You keep spoiling him he'll always be a baby!" his father said when he found Joey in their mother's room, the flowered bedspread pulled over his head. His father's voice was firm and clear in his head.

Joey realized his body was shaking.

"Are you there, Joseph?" It was Patricia. "Joseph?"

He unlocked his hands from around his knees.

"You looked like part of the house," she said. Her laugh, high and nervous, floated into him. "I'm so glad you came."

She came close and touched his shoulder. Her dark hair fell straight against her cheeks, thinning her face. She wore a coat that blended with the shadows and she held it close.

"Neville and I are getting married." Her words came in a rush. "He asked me and I said yes before I lost him again." She paused, "I know mother would have liked him."

"Did he know what you were planning?" Joey asked, and imagined his father's temper, the shouting and the angry words.

"Neville wouldn't come here." Patricia's voice trailed off and in its place was the racket of crickets. "The fire started in mother's room."

"In mother's room?" Joey asked.

"There was nothing father could do." Patricia paused. "He yelled at the flames, at the firemen, at God. It was his heart just gave out."

Joey stared at the wedge of blackened chimney. He still found it hard to believe.

"We can start again. Neville and I can build our own place now, right over this foundation." She touched Joey's shoulder. "You can come and live with us then."

"I can't come back." He was learning a trade in Sydney, to make cabinets with fine scrolled legs and inlaid doors, hope chests with ornate hearts carved in the lids.

"You can work with Dave Henderson, building houses." Patricia's tone reminded him of their father's voice when he wanted something. "Dave's going to build our house, Neville's and mine."

Joey stood and stretched. His whole body ached. There was no way he could come back and build houses here. "Patricia?" he asked. "How did the fire start?"

"I'm thinking of taking a job," she continued, "Maybe help at the school or the town library, they always need volunteers." She paused and patted Joey's shoulder, "After the funeral is done, of course." She turned and walked briskly back up the path toward Mrs. Worthy's house, calling over her shoulder. "We have so much to do, Joey. Are you coming?"

He watched her disappear, watched the lights winking through the trees as the evening wind picked up and caught the leaves. He felt chilled, felt a new ache settle in his chest as he followed her.

Waiting for Queenie

Marty arrived at the diner around 6:00 a.m., before the first batch of coffee soured. He came to have breakfast and to see Queenie. With her bouncy hair and bright eyes, her full hips moving smoothly under her short black skirt, she had a way of making a customer feel important. They had a nice relationship; he brought her the latest news from the Sydney Herald he picked up on the way, and she brought him coffee and muffins.

Queenie reminded Marty of other women he'd known. Like Sally who worked at the Churchill Pub; both of them had thick dark hair, wide hips. And before Sally he'd spent evenings with Adele in Murphy's Tavern. He never asked those women out, not women as busy as they were. He liked their company, to sit and talk the evenings away discussing world events, the headlines. Now he liked someone's company in the mornings, at the start of the day, when the newspapers were fresh and smelled of printer's ink.

Queenie was busy when he settled in his seat by the door. He waited as she filled mugs, picked up empty plates, wiped down the counter.

"How you doing, Marty?" she asked, coffee pot raised in her hand. "You ready?" She called all the customers by their surnames, except for him, and he liked that sense of intimacy.

"Morning Queenie," he said. "You hear about the child nearly drowned, little fellow saved by his Mum?" He pointed to the headline.

She poured his coffee without losing a drop. "Miracles happen, Marty."

"You're so right, Queenie." He was eager to have her stay. "Last night there was a drug bust in Paddington." He spread the newspaper on the counter so she could see the grainy photo of police cars and fire engines.

"Imagine," she shrugged, "A posh place like that?"

"And there was a shoot-out in some cinema in America," He paused to remember the details. "Twelve dead, seven wounded."

"What can you expect in this crazy world?"

"And a woman fell on top of her friend to save her," he said. "She took the bullet."

"Really?" She put her hand on the open newspaper. "It's not often you hear someone cares for someone else like that."

He wanted to take her hand and say, "Hey! I'm here, aren't I? Every morning I'm here because of you." He worked at the reference desk in the City Library answering questions all day, working with the public. It was lonely though; people moved on quickly once they had the answers they were looking for. He was happy to linger over his coffee, and he liked Queenie's company, the time they spent together.

Queenie returned with his warmed over muffins, two pats of butter.

Marty had the paper open to show her the photo of the plane crash in Germany. Queenie would be intrigued, but the front door opened with a rush of fresh air and Rayburn, another regular, walked through. "Hallo gorgeous," he called to Queenie.

"And good morning to you!" she replied.

"Be back in a minute," she said to Marty. These days she barely stood still long enough to hear what he was saying. Wars threatened in the Middle East, gun violence escalating in America, Muslims taking over whole Sydney suburbs, and Queenie was showing less interest.

Rayburn took his usual seat at the end of the counter. He was long in the body and wore a baseball hat low on his head with Simms Electrics printed on the front. His red checkered jacket was zipped halfway up his broad chest.

"You got some fresh for me, Queenie?" Marty heard Rayburn ask. The man talked like he was used to giving orders, of being in charge.

"I'll make a new pot," she tossed her hair and moved the little jug of milk nearer his hands. How could she be so pleasant to such a man?

The clock on the wall told Marty he had another half hour before he had to get the computers up and read his e-mail. He folded his newspaper to the crossword, readied his ballpoint pen, and another regular walked in.

"Morning everyone," Larry Smelts called to the room at large. He sat between Marty and Rayburn, two stools apart. He was square and chunky, with a ruddy face and sandy hair thinning. He seemed too young for that patch of light skin but he didn't cover it with a cap.

Smelts saw Queenie with the coffee pot, "Got some for me, love?" His voice was low and easy going.

Those two men came around the same time Marty did. There were other customers, of course, sitting in the booths along the far wall, at tables under the windows, others who came and left quickly, but only the three regulars lingered. He never did hear Rayburn's first name, everyone just called him Rayburn. And Smelts was sometimes Larry when Joe, the manager of the diner poked his head out to check how the service was going. Queenie called him Smelts, just like she called the big man Rayburn. It gave her greetings a formal quality, set a distance between her and them, or that's what Marty believed.

"You catch the Parramatta Eels game last night?" Rayburn asked Queenie. He watched all the games on TV except when they played a home match and he bought tickets. He was full of wins and losses, kept all the scores in his head. "You coming with me to the home game, Queenie?" His voice was loud enough for Marty to hear, along with most of the other customers.

"If I wasn't so busy, I'd come," she said swinging a tea towel over her shoulder. "Maybe the finals," she said with a smile. "Remind me."

Smelts voice was softer. "Good coffee this morning, Queenie," he said, cup raised for another fill. "Have you seen the latest *Mission Impossible*?" He put both feet on the stool's metal ring. "That little Cruise fellow can run," he shook his head. He talked about the funny shows on TV, the latest films and possible Oscar nominations. Marty had to strain to hear what he was saying. One morning Marty heard Smelts ask, "So, how's Jimmy?"

"Glad you asked," Queenie answered. She dropped her voice, leaned in, and Marty missed the rest of the conversation.

Jimmy? Marty checked Queenie's left hand in case there was a new ring on her finger. Nothing, so who was Jimmy? He wondered if he could ask her but it wasn't his conversation.

He stared out the window. Queenie swung by and Marty snapped to. "You bake these muffins? They're delicious."

"You think I have time?" she pushed back her hair. She gave the counter an absent-minded swipe and poured the coffee so fast it splashed on the counter.

"Not my day," she said, wiping up the mess.

"You hear about the train crash in Newcastle, Queenie?" He had the paper open, the photo ready, the precise number of passengers taken to the local hospital, but she was gone through the swing doors into the kitchen. She returned with plates of food balanced on her arm for the table of four seated under the window.

"You hear about the Eels game last Saturday, Queenie?" Rayburn's big hands played with the salt and pepper shakers, made them circle each other like a pair of sparring fighters. "Game turned on a bad call."

Smelts held up his coffee cup. He rarely put his hands on the counter, kept them out of sight when he wasn't drinking or eating.

"Coming," she called, pushing through the kitchen door.

Marty felt ignored. He should leave, find another diner. Or ask Queenie out. Other men did, but he never seemed to quite get to a place in the relationship where he could. He couldn't put his finger on why that was.

"You want a fill?" Queenie was standing there with the coffee pot, frown lines on her forehead. Marty nodded.

Queenie headed for the kitchen, her hand on the swing door. "Queenie, love, you got some more sugar out there?" She paused, shot Smelts a weary smile, "Sure, be right back." Queenie returned with a handful of sugar packets and filled the container.

"Thanks, love," Smelts said.

She came back to Marty. "You want something more than coffee this morning?" Her voice was snappy. There was a time when Queenie was pleased to talk to him, wanted to talk to him. They'd been close, like Sally and he were close before she told him she was engaged to some fellow who ran a taxicab. Like Adele told him she was married, but not wearing her wedding ring. Queenie was different, had been different.

Marty wanted to say, *Will you just stop for a moment and listen to me?*

"You want something more than coffee and muffin this morning?"

"No," he said quickly. She'd embarrassed him. He knew the other regulars ordered large meals. Big meals meant big tips. Marty thought he could order more, maybe an egg on toast with a side of bacon. Maybe that was the trouble between him and Queenie. The small tips he left for her.

"Ready to order," Smelts called. "Two eggs over easy, bacon, side of pancakes." He ate his breakfast slowly, savoring each mouthful until the plate was clean.

Queenie brought Rayburn his French toast with sausage and chips. "Smells good this morning," Rayburn set the toast swimming in syrup.

It was a morning like every other until Rayburn grabbed Queenie's wrist. The sleeve of his jacket caught the silverware and sent it flying. Conversation stopped and diners craned to see what the noise was about.

"Don't do that," Queenie's voice was clear.

Smelts looked up, alert. "You okay, Queenie?"

Queenie opened her mouth to say something and Rayburn let her wrist go. So sudden she was left without a reply. Not a smile or a wink or a smart sassy word like Marty expected to hear. Smelts was leaning forward in his seat so he could see past the two customers between him and Rayburn, straining to see better. Marty realized the two men each talked to Queenie and Queenie talked to them, but they never spoke to each other.

Queenie moved into the kitchen. Smelts set his elbow on the counter, turned his body slightly on the stool. Marty saw his face clearly, drawn and set, older, like his partially balding head.

On the last Friday in June, around 2:30 p.m., Marty came down Stebbins Street, thinking of Queenie. If he needed to leave the City Library for any reason he took Anderson Avenue, the route was shorter to the dry cleaners, yet here he was on Stebbins Street like some lost homing pigeon. He rounded the corner and two doorways up from the diner he saw them— Queenie, big Rayburn and Smelts.

He drew back into the doorway of the apartment block holding his plastic bag full of soiled shirts against his side. It was a shock to see that tight triangle of figures on the footpath.

Queenie had a hand on Rayburn's shoulder and her other hand on Smelts' arm like she was pushing them apart. The two men were talking at each other, faces thrust forward like two over-sized fighting cocks. Queenie was keeping them apart, her face swinging from one to the other and her mouth was open as though she was trying to eat their words.

"Leave us alone, Queenie!" Rayburn's voice, loud and plain.

"Stop it!" Queenie shouted. She pushed at Rayburn and his cap fell off.

Rayburn grabbed Smelts' shirt. "I said I was taking her to the game!" he shouted. He looked at Queenie. "Tell him that's the way we decided, Queenie."

Smelts was focused on Queenie's face. Rayburn had a handful of his shirt and Smelts had to tilt his head above Rayburn's big fist.

"Queenie wouldn't be seen dead with you," Rayburn shouted. Rayburn shook Smelts by his shirtfront. "Queenie, tell him!"

"She's going with me." Smelts said. His voice was distorted by the pressure of Rayburn's hand. "We've set the date."

Marty froze. Set the date! Marriage? Not his Queenie. Not with Smelts. What had he missed all those mornings?

Rayburn swayed. He pushed Smelts into the brick wall and Marty heard the dull thud. His back hit and hung there for a moment. Smelts gripped his throat and slid down the wall.

"You're a bully, that's all you are." Queenie seemed small beside Rayburn. "A loud-mouthed bully!" Rayburn took hold of her hands and she pulled away. "Let go of me!"

Marty's chest hurt like he had serious heartburn. Was he having a heart attack? He felt ill as Rayburn glared at Queenie. "You've been seeing us both," Rayburn stated flatly. "You've been seeing him," he flicked his thumb at Smelts, "while you've been seeing me." Smelts looked like a punching bag that had been beaten once too often.

"You don't listen," Queenie answered. "Larry's like a father to Jimmy now."

Jimmy? A son? She'd never told Marty she had a son.

"You're one dumb broad," Rayburn shouted. "Dumb!" He smacked Queenie, and she fell against Smelts. Marty's heart hammered in his chest. Rayburn was going to hit her again.

Hit his Queenie! He pressed his body tighter against the brick wall. His breath came in little gasps. Should he intervene? Show Queenie he could protect her from a bully like Rayburn?

"So you've set the date?" Rayburn sneered. "Well, good luck to you both."

Queenie wrapped her arms around Smelts' shoulders like she was hugging a child. Rayburn stared at them for another moment and walked off. He marched down Stebbins Street, arms swinging, away from where Marty was hiding.

How could Queenie betray him like that? She was no different than Sally or Adele or any other woman he'd cared about. Marty had read about betrayal in the newspapers every day, about violence on the streets, about men beating up women, women leaving men, fickle women. But his Queenie?

Marty slid from the doorway and walked back the way he'd come. Forget the dry cleaning. Forget Queenie. There were other woman out there waiting for his friendship. He just had to find another place for his morning coffee and muffins.

Guv'ment Lady

Henrietta Doyle was clearing weeds from around her prized hollyhocks when the postman arrived at the back fence. Her knees were stiff from kneeling on the uneven ground, and she struggled a little to stand. It bothered her to think she'd soon need a stool or a walking stick.

"An official-looking envelope for you, Miss Doyle!" George Hume called.

"Thank you, George." She took the letter and smiled in dismissal. Other than her father's pension check, which arrived each month in a brown envelope, Henrietta rarely received mail.

The Department of Railways, Sydney, was stamped in brilliant black lettering on the envelope, with the Seal of State at the side. Her name was formally typed in full: Henrietta Abigail Doyle. Very official. Inside the house, she automatically glanced at the open door of the corner room. "Well, open it up," her father would have bellowed from the side bedroom. "Get the letter opener and find out what it says."

The letter was a formal request for Henrietta to supervise the opening and closing of the company gates that were soon to be installed at the rail crossing near her house. "Owing to the fact that your father was an esteemed employee of the railways…." She read to the end. There had been an accident, it explained, forty miles down the train line, four people had been killed when the train hit their truck. Gates were to be installed at all rail crossings on the Southern line to prevent such accidents from happening again.

They were offering her a job. She reread the letter slowly. They would pay her, too. A godsend, given her father's pension barely covered her needs and the compost for her garden.

There was little traffic in town, so she could do the job easily and have the privilege of working where her father had worked, for the government. "Government!" How important it would sound when she spoke to the ladies in her knitting group. And, Tom Carpenter would be pleased with her news. He was one of the brotherhood, a rail worker, and now the master cabman once her father retired. The thought of Tom lifted her spirits further.

Tom had been here that evening two weeks before her father died. He was here with several other railmen, gathered round his bed, sitting awkwardly in chairs, the room so small their knees were touching. They were sharing stories and her father retold the one about Franklin's prize bull. "There it was. Dead center on the tracks." He'd paused to cough. "Was there anything I could do?" He asked, and the men waited patiently for the punch line. "No!" He answered. "Franklin had been warned." There was laughter then. They understood.

Henrietta decided to post her acceptance letter that day and pick up some groceries at the same time. She wore her favorite hat with its small bunch of artificial cherries in the band against the fierceness of the late spring sun. Cicadas shrieked from the wattle trees and dust floated knee-high against her skirt as she walked up the unpaved road. She reached Nolan's shop and paused at the wire-screened door. Flies buzzed against the warm front window, climbed and fell to crawl along the windowsill. Ethel Lynch was leaning on the wooden counter, a bag of groceries cradled in her thick arms. Ethel was the last person she wanted to see.

"He was there again last night!" Ethel's chin jutted with the latest gossip. "Saw the lights of his car clear through the trees. And those dogs of hers! They should be put down for their barking."

Alma Nolan, owner of the shop, stood sturdily behind the wooden counter.

Ethel stretched out her hand for the change. "I can't get a decent night's sleep these days."

Henrietta pushed through the door and the conversation stopped.

Alma continued to count out Ethel's change, "You're right," she murmured. "Taking in more milk, she is." She clapped the money drawer shut. Ethel turned.

"Such a lovely funeral." Ethel directed the comment to Henrietta as she came through the door. "...and the flowers."

The glibness of her words, such a lovely funeral! Indecent after the bitter fight her father had had with Ethel to gain evening hours at the town library, Ethel maliciously dividing the town over his request and her father sick at the time.

Alma straightened the daily papers on the counter. "We don't see much of you these days, Henrietta. Busy with the garden?"

The garden reminded her of her letter. "The government..." Henrietta began.

"I was saying," Ethel broke in. "Something's going on in the street at the back of you, Henrietta. With Nell the way she is, simple and such-like, it's a real sin it is." Ethel's voice was impressively righteous.

"I feel badly for Nell," Henrietta leaned past Ethel and gathered up her paper. "Some men have no conscience."

Ethel's face tightened. "I can't imagine you'd agree with Nell having a baby year after year, each with a different daddy. It's not Christian!" She stared at Henrietta with narrowed eyes. "If it's Bluey Grant again, he should be run out of town."

"Can't be Bluey," put in Alma, folding her arms. "He works night shifts down at the gravel plant."

"Then it's one of his friends," Ethel shot back.

Henrietta felt hollowed out by the heat, the constant droning of flies. Ethel Lynch was out to make trouble as always. "It's a blue truck goes down the track of an evening," Henrietta said. "Someone in a blue truck has been visiting Nell these nights."

Ethel straightened abruptly, the bag of groceries clutched in her arms.

The strip of flypaper curling from the ceiling above Alma's head twisted in the sudden movement of air.

"Well, I never," Alma spoke as the screened door snapped shut. "You certainly gave Ethel a start, and her boy Freddy the only one in town owns a blue truck."

"I'll take some cornflakes and four apples," Henrietta said.

"You were saying about the government?" Alma asked.

Remembering her letter, Henrietta explained its contents. She described the elegance of the state seal, the heft of the paper, the fact that she would be paid.

"The department of railways, fancy that! Wouldn't your father be proud?" Alma flattened the bills and slipped them out of sight. "Not that there's much traffic here in the morning, but you can't be too careful, can you?"

Henrietta picked up her dilly bag. Alma's interest was most gratifying. She regretted the store was empty but could rest in the knowledge that Alma would quickly pass on her news.

The following morning, Henrietta opened the back door of her house and found a brown paper bag had been placed on the top step. Tom Carpenter often left her something from his garden, a few carrots, some chard, brussel sprouts, so she was not surprised. He visited every Friday night now she was alone, and this past Friday she had baked her new lamb kidney casserole. "Delicious, Hettie, how do you do it?" he'd said as they sipped a glass of port together and discussed her new job.

Inside the paper bag was an untidy roll of stained butcher's paper, and when she pulled it apart, something hairy dropped to the floor. The head of a rat. Its jaws were open, and she saw its sharp yellow teeth. Dried blood specked the fur. One eye gleamed nastily.

"Dear God," she covered her mouth with her hands. Who would ever leave such a thing? It was disgusting but the truth dawned on her—only Freddy! It had to be Freddy Lynch.

She gathered her gardening gloves from the kitchen drawer and disposed of the parcel. Then she took down her father's brandy and poured a glass. He would have shared her anger. Pulling himself up on the pillows, he'd say, "He'll get his come-uppance, Hettie. Just you wait, they always get their come-uppance!" She could hear his voice clearly. Henrietta sipped her brandy. She missed her father; two months was too short a time to be done with grieving.

Ten days later Henrietta walked up the road and watched the workmen set the posts at the rail crossing and roll out the new gates from the back of their van. The gates swung smoothly on their new hinges and she felt a surge of pride at her upcoming responsibility.

A truck drove up behind her. "How's it going, Miss Doyle?" Freddy used a childish sing-song voice as he leaned through the side window. "Be seeing you on the way to work these mornings, I hear." His eyes were small and hostile under his cap.

"I don't want any nonsense, Freddy," Henrietta replied sharply. "I have a job to do for the government."

"Guv'ment!" Freddy grinned. "We mustn't make trouble for the guv'ment lady!" He revved his engine. "I had any trouble with rats lately, Miss Doyle?" He slapped the steering wheel and, laughing loudly, drove off in a burst of grey smoke.

Henrietta told Tom about this latest affront when he came to supper that Friday.

A week later, her responsibilities began. It was a fine morning. She walked across the tracks and pulled the far gate closed, retraced her steps and swung the near gate into its metal latch. A horn beeped down the road. The train came into view over the rise and barreled by between the gates, the great pumping pistons hissing and churning, soot-laden smoke hot on her cheeks. Tom Carpenter leaned from the engine's cabin and waved a blackened hand, a broad grin on his face.

The train receded up the track, and the insistent honking of Freddy's horn came from behind her. She unfastened the first gate to bring it back, but Freddy had driven so close there was no room for it to swing free. She could touch the glossy silver emblem on the hood of his truck: a jungle cat leaping upwards, its front paws reaching forward into space. How typical of

Freddy to have an emblem of a predator, she thought, obviously stolen from someone's racy car. "Back up, Freddy!" she called.

He cupped his hand to his ear. She came to the cabin door. The window was high off the ground, so she banged on the blue metal. Freddy took his time in winding down the window.

"Need some help, Miss Doyle?" He looked down at her.

"Move your truck back, Freddy!" She shouted to be heard over the engine's racket. "I can't open the gate!"

The truck rolled back in a leisurely fashion, and Henrietta let the gate swing to the fence. She walked up and over the railway tracks to unlatch the other gate, and the blue truck nosed along behind her until the second gate clicked into its post then roared away.

In the mornings that followed, Freddy and she were alone together at the gates to witness the train's passing. He always waited until the far gate was swung to and latched and she walked back over the rails to push the near gate closed. He raced the motor, rocked the truck forward and backwards, edged it ever nearer to her as she waited for the train to pass. At times there was barely room for her to turn between the shiny barred gate and the hot metal fender. It was frightening: the heated closeness of the truck, Freddy's smirking face behind the windscreen, the memory of the rat's head.

The following Monday morning, she started for the crossing in a grimly pleasant mood. Freddy would be warned that her patience had reached its limit, that she would no longer tolerate his nonsense, that she would report him to the authorities. But to her surprise, Freddy's truck was nowhere to be seen. As the train clattered by, Tom Carpenter leaned from the engine's cab, waved to Henrietta and tipped his cap. Still Freddy had not arrived.

She worked in her garden and thought about Freddy's absence. She transplanted a clump of impatiens that was suffocating the newly established bachelor's buttons, and put in a dozen zinnias to cover the hole. She gathered up her dilly bag that afternoon, made a list of her needs, and walked up the road to the shop.

Alma Nolan was checking through the boxes of vegetables, throwing the spoiled cucumbers and tomatoes, squash and cabbage, into a pail at her feet. Lou Winter's hogs would eat well that evening. "Morning," Alma said breathlessly, wiping her hands on her apron where the stains of her present chore were all too obvious. "Has the job gone well, Henrietta?" Alma had an air of excitement about her, a glow in her cheeks.

"Very well, indeed," she replied crisply. "And how is Ethel these days? And Freddy?" She packed her dilly bag with the groceries Alma placed before her.

"But haven't you heard?" Alma gripped the counter and leaned forward, eyes checking the door. "Ethel's in an awful state. Stayed here talking all morning. She's going to the police today if no word comes of him." Alma's hands twisted on the edge of her apron. "Home on Saturday, he was, went out later to drink with his mates at the pub and never came home!"

Black flies buzzed on the cloudy window pane.

"But," Alma leaned back and folded her arms on her apron bib. "Old Sid was in first thing this morning and he said Freddy's truck was left on the main line sometime on Saturday night. When the freight train came through, it smashed the truck to pieces." Alma paused. "Makes you wonder where Freddy was to leave his truck there like that?"

Henrietta sighed. That explained it all. A large beef roast sat on the refrigerated shelf of the meat counter along with some sausages and lamb chops. She knew now why Freddy and his blue truck hadn't bothered her this morning. "I'll have a nice lean roast for the end of the week," she said to Alma, "and a bag of onions and three parsnips." Tom Carpenter deserved the best when he came to dinner on Friday night.

The Pink Wall

Gotta trash this wall! Put a hole in it, a real big hole I can walk through. Just line it up, middle of the wall where the watermark is the shape of a duck's foot, down from the nail hole and between the studs.

This room always was safe. No one looks in on me here. Just a closet really, big old chair, shelf to put my feet on. Used to be restful; not knowing time, no sun to watch, nothing 'cept the odd fly comes in on my back. I could sit here with a bottle of beer, hear the sounds of the house, her feet sometimes, but mostly listen to the blood pumping in my throat. Fights are what bring me here, lock myself away. Fists so tight they cramp, nails break the skin, tight as that.

Expect she's calling to me, expect she'll be coming sometime soon, feeling badly for what she done, and I'll wait, see how I fix her after she's come back. This was my daddy's house and here O'Brian's telling me to leave, tells me the fire's pushing up the gully. And Margy's packed the suitcase. One moment we're yelling at each other, the next I'm waiting in this room for her to come get me.

There's gotta be time. My cheek's swelling like a football from the bottle she threw. The way we fight now everything's changed. She's strong, gets the better of me. Used to be I was the strongest, but no more. The other day we were fighting, I looked aways from her and back, she's got a broom in her hands, mean look on her face. I try to drag the broom away, she pulls back, nearly yanks my arms off.

"You don't hit me again, old man," she says. "Never again, you hear?" She stands her ground, broom raised at me, I see her piggy eyes, her lips stretched into her cheeks like the zipper on her empty purse.

This wall, flat little wall in my room, can't see nothing beyond. Not a blade of grass, sky, or the fence runs along O'Brian's. Chops the meadow up, that fence. Three wire strands running post to post, cows push their heads through, rip it loose. They're my cows. Need to put an electric fence there, stop them dead—but the goddam money. Let him put some money down, half of it's his anyways.

O'Brian now, queer old coot, woman-of-a-man watching us, and he don't wave no more to me. He puts an extra strand of barbed wire in the other week, along the top of the fence. Didn't ask me, says it's for the cows, likely thought to keep me out, too. O'Brian, with his bantam strut, some cocky scoutmaster-type, polishes his boots. See him staring at my woman, see him squinting through the fence over to my side when she pegs out the clothes. Know what you're thinking O'Brian, six years since your old biddy up and left you. Margy's too young for both of us old 'uns, so full of juice makes for tender takings, but she's mine, O'Brian.

I caught you talking to her a while back, swung the axe to my shoulder, marched over to you both by the fence. "You got something to say O'Brian?" I scuttled him good! Turned once, he did, as he crossed his lettuce beds, red-faced. He understood the axe in my hands. He's seen me hit the hair-crack in a log, two, three times, clean on, no missing.

That wall now, a picture hung there once; flat black trees and a red-roofed barn, animals in that picture. Wasn't no fire, though. Don't know why the picture got put there, only a storage room, shelves down one side, no windows. Picture came down years ago, can't remember where it got put then, some cupboard, maybe she locked it in some cupboard.

Picture musta come down seven years ago when Margy was eight, going nine, musta been. Back when she had braids, stringy things, and nothing under her sweater but smooth skin. Knew I'd have her even then, watching her go by to school, growing all the time. Her knowing I was watching. Living out this end of Five-Mile Road, track really, her shack at the end, my place up aways, next door was Simpson and his old woman. They die, O'Brian comes along. Not the same since O'Brian moved in.

I can hear trucks revving, lots of noise coming through the wall, gears changing, somebody shouting. Can't see through this wall to check my hearing's right, see across the fence, the barbed wire. Something's going on over in O'Brian's yard and Margy must be there.

I could break this wall down soon as look at it, if I wanted. Still got my strength. Make a mark there with one of the pencil stubs Margy left behind when she was a kid. Used those iddy-bits of pencil when she was little, drew pictures for me on the front porch, on her way home from school, going down to her shack and her good-for-nothing kin. "Hallo, mister," she'd say, shy-like, not fretting I was older than her father.

Anyway, I don't need no mark. Don't matter if the hole isn't straight on, measured up right, even spaced with the studs. Just need a hole is all. Getting hot in here now, have to lay my clothes off. Shirt and undershirt, shoes, ain't wearing no socks. That hole now. All that cool air rushing in on my face. Stick both hands through the hole if it's big enough, feel the wind on my knuckles, open my hands, maybe feel rain falling on my palms, trickling 'tween my fingers. Imaginings! Like my mama used to say about the bunyipman coming to get me, sneaking up from the gully, climbing in the window, reaching under the blanket for me. "Stop all that nonsense!" she'd say. "I'll thrash you, you don't go to sleep."

There's no hole and there's no rain out there. Long time ago since I've had water in my hands and liked it. I took Margy down to the creek once, early spring it was, and the creek running fast, spilling over the rocks, coming down the sides of the gully in a rush. Those blue flowers everywhere! Margy called them billy-goat orchids for the furry petal hanging like a twist of beard. She picked some. Made a pesky pile on my shorts, brought them home, 'cept they were all crushed. Maybe she was too young for what I done, had to seal her to me, be the first. Didn't give her no time to argue, her body so small I went easy. She didn't fight me then. Found I wasn't the first. Could have killed her old man but he was gone to Wagga Wagga.

Lunchtime today, it was, we had the big fight. And me drinking beer 'til I didn't know which way was up. She's matching me one for one, but it don't do nothing to her. Saw the fire aways off, glow in the gully and smoke rising up in a sheet of grey from the eucalypts. Those trees smoke like chimney stacks when they light. Tad of wind makes it look worse'n it is. Told me in the local store this morning when I got those six-packs, bush fire's coming along from Balmoral, scooting up the gullies where the trees are like tinder, this drought and all. "Watch for it," they said, as I got my smokes. "Being in its path there on the ridge, you tell O'Brian watch it!"

We had alarms like this when I was a kid. Years ago they put in a firebreak, below our place and wide, bulldozer felled trees all week like they were matchsticks. Old man said we'd be safe. "No fire can jump that break, son!" he said. Too many years have gone, firebreaks overgrown some, no one keeping it cleared. Should hold good though, the old man said they'd last forever. Leaving my daddy's house's not easy for me, and the fire's going to be stopped, was stopped before. People'll come, or the wind'll change, like it happened in the big fire of '71.

Lunchtime when I come home from the shop, we fight. I hit her. She hits me back. Times like this I worry she's so fierce with her back against the table, spitting when she yells like her mouth can't move round her words, mouth open and her tongue an angry pink.

"Go on!" she screams. "Go on into that room of yours. I'll lock the goddam door and throw away the key!"

"Yeah!" I shout at her. "You do that and I'll snap your neck like it was a chicken's ready for Christmas plucking!" *Crazy bitch!*

"I'll see you in hell first!" she throws a bottle at the wall.

Her voice goes on and on, rings in my head. I can't stand it no more so I back away from her and she hits me with one of those flying bottles. *Smack!* on the side of the cheek, nearly takes my ear off. "Bitch!" I kick over a chair, make room to teach her a lesson good and there's calling at the back door.

O'Brian's there, on the top step, knocking and hollering how it's time to move or we'll be fried. "Fire's strong enough to jump the clearing," he yells.

I see bits of burned leaf in his hair, cheeks spotted with ash, don't mean nothing. Wind carries ash miles from a fire. "Stuff you!" I say to them both. "I'm not leaving yet."

"You wanna stay?" And Margy slaps the table with her hand. "Then stay! But I'm going!" Then she's heading out the door and O'Brian's staring at me and the table full of empties, staring at me like I've lost my mind or something.

"You coming?" he yells, backing down the steps, making room for Margy. She's got the brown suitcase in her hand tied with my piece of rope. Didn't know she'd packed, done it behind my back like she does everything now.

"You go in that room," she says from the top step, and she don't raise her voice none. "You're dead!"

"Don't sass me girl," I say. "I'll be coming when I'm good and ready, not when you say."

Didn't want O'Brian to think she bossed me round, skin on my cheek grazed, him knowing we'd been fighting. There'll be time to think what I'll do to her and that bug-eyed little weasel when I'm ready. O'Brian and Margy kicking up a fuss, using this to get off together; she can pack her things without me knowing, she can have something on with O'Brian.

I'll give them maybe five more minutes before I come, show them who's in charge. This room now, it's peaceful here. I feel the swelling on my face, start to think on what I'll do and I hear the key turn in the lock, a sharp click, loud as a whip cracking. Takes me a moment to understand what's happened.

"What're you doing?" I yell. "Margy! That you?"

I try the doorknob. I put my ear to the door but I don't hear nothing, no trucks, no shouting, no footsteps. I pound on the wood, pound 'til my arms ache and the door holds tight like it's made for eternity. So I sit here and wait in my daddy's house, figuring how to break out, break Margy's neck. The room's beginning to heat more. Could be the wall is burning, turning pinkly rose like the inside of her mouth.

A Flower for Malcolm

Lena Temple heard her husband's heels hit the oak boards of the hallway. He paused at the front door to straighten his tie before the glass panel and adjust the handkerchief in his breast pocket to a narrow white strip.

"I have to go," he called.

"I'm coming!" Lena pulled a frangipani blossom from the glass vase on the dining room table. She wiped the wet stem on her skirt.

"Where were you?" He offered his lapel.

"Will you be home for supper tonight?" She held up the pale, cream-colored flower. Frangipani trees planted in old cemeteries were called the *flower of the dead*. Perhaps, Lena thought, it was time to change the flower in Malcolm's buttonhole.

She slipped her hand under his lapel and positioned the frangipani stem. He pursed his lips. His pink bottom lip protruded under the tight line of the upper one. The unexpected shape of his mouth had always intrigued Lena.

"I'll be late tonight, another meeting." He touched her cheek where the skin was grazed.

Business was doing very well and they had taken on some new staff to cope with the heavy demand. "Fortunately," Malcolm had told her with a smile, "everyone needs some form of insurance." Lena would meet these new employees at Friday's gathering of co-investors.

"We had another of those phone calls," she said.

Malcolm picked up his briefcase. "They don't leave a name?"

"There's music in the background," Lena said. The fragment of music she'd heard had piqued her imagination. Brubeck, perhaps? She and

Malcolm had enjoyed the nightclubs in Kings Cross back in their courting days; enjoyed the jazz bands, the sax, the muted trumpets, the throbbing of the double bass. Brubeck had been his favorite in those days.

"They hang up before I can ask for a name."

"You think it's for me?" Malcolm asked. "Next time, give them my work number."

During lunch the telephone rang and this time it was her sister. "Norman's left again," Margaret said abruptly. "He's been depressed and I don't want Poppy here. She asks too many questions."

Norman was never happy. He was always complaining—about his job, or the weather, or the time he spent doing the lawn.

"Please take her." Margaret sounded tired. "There's nowhere else she can go."

"Shouldn't she be in school?" Lena thought of the empty house and her sister pacing the rooms, of Poppy waiting by the door for her father's return. "Never mind, I love Poppy. Send her down."

"It's all such a mess."

"You know where he's gone?" Lena asked.

"He took a bag of clothes and his electric shaver." This wasn't the first time Norman had run off but each time Margaret worried it could be the last.

"Does he want a divorce again?"

"He just left." Margaret replied with a sigh. "They're calling from work and I've said he has the flu."

"He'll be back," Lena assured her. "He'll just walk through the door again and you'll pick up where you left off."

What else was there to say; people gossiped. Norman was artistic, immature, always had been, and her sister was a romantic. Malcolm seemed so dependable by comparison though Margaret might be surprised at how imaginative he could be.

"Margaret?" Lena asked. "Have you been trying to call me?"

"No. Why?"

"Nothing, the phone rings sometimes and when I answer the line goes dead." Lena laughed. "It couldn't be Norman?"

"Not likely." Margaret hung up.

Poppy arrived by train at Central Station. She was nine years old and looked completely lost in the middle of the busy station. She faced the clock tower, with her feet straddling a worn suitcase. There were traces of chocolate in the corners of her mouth. "Aunt Lena?" she called and ran into Lena's arms. "Daddy's gone," she said.

"He'll be home soon," Lena reassured her. "It's so good to have you visit." And she hugged Poppy closer. "Grab your bag and we'll find the car."

The following day, Lena stood in the hallway and checked the time on her neat square wristwatch. She'd have to attend to her skirt if she was to wear it on Friday, dining with Malcolm's colleagues. "Poppy, we have errands to do!" Lena swung the pot-bellied kettle off the hotplate and stood it in the sink to be cleaned; she cleared Malcolm's breakfast dishes and set a place for her niece.

"I'm coming," Poppy answered, running down the hallway. "I'm starved," she said as she sat down. "I heard Uncle Malcolm leave."

"An egg?" Lena asked, putting one on to boil.

"Yes, please." Poppy fidgeted on the chair.

"The zipper in my favorite skirt is torn," Lena placed the boiled egg before Poppy. She cooked the perfect egg, three minutes and a bit. "It needs some invisible mending." Lena took the teakettle and started scrubbing off the baked-on stains.

"Mummy spilt some hot water on daddy the other day." Poppy wagged her spoon at Lena. "He was very, very cross!"

"I imagine he would be!" So that was part of the story, maybe one reason for Norman's abrupt leaving. Malcolm would be furious if that happened to him.

When Poppy finished her egg, she turned it upside down. "I'm finished," she said with a little giggle.

"Finished?" asked Lena.

A perfect white egg sat in the china cup. Lena rapped on the eggshell. Hollow little taps. Poppy enjoyed the shared moment; she slid off the chair and took the basket Lena handed her. Licking the last traces of butter from her fingers she twirled around the kitchen floor, coming down with her two feet together.

"Did you hear that, Aunt Lena?" Poppy asked. "My feet came down together. I listen to people's feet. Everyone's footsteps sound different."

Lena's high heels tapped over the kitchen floorboards.

"Uncle Malcolm walks like this," Poppy said, holding herself stiffly and putting her shoes down precisely, squarely on the floor. "I heard him this morning, coming down the hall."

"Your uncle was going to work," Lena said.

"My father walks like this in the morning," Poppy shuffled her feet. "I don't think he'll ever come back."

"Of course he'll come back," Lena said. "Sometimes we just need to change old habits."

Poppy stopped and folded her arms across her body. "He doesn't have the flu like mummy says."

Lena folded the tea towel and hung it on the oven door. "It must be terribly confusing for you."

"Mummy says not to ask questions." She stared into Lena's face. "I don't understand anything about grown-ups."

"I didn't understand them at your age."

"He could be dead," Poppy said mournfully.

"Don't be silly, Poppy. He'll come home by the end of the week."

"Do you think so?" Poppy swung the empty basket against her legs. "Aunt Lena, your skirt?"

Of course, the skirt! "I'll get it," she said heading for their bedroom.

She gathered up the skirt and there was the newspaper she'd been reading last night lying on the floor beside the bed. She spread the paper flat on the sheets and reread the short article with its half-inch headline and grainy photograph. A woman had locked her husband outside their house and while he banged on the front door, she leaned from the upstairs window and poured a kettle of boiling water over his head. A painful little story, something she wouldn't have glanced at in the past but for Poppy's story. There was so much turmoil out in the world. The photo showed the man sitting on the front steps with his face buried in a towel while the woman stood to the side holding a large black kettle. Marriage was such a fragile arrangement.

Lena checked her hair in the mirror and ran her fingers down the side of her face over the faint bruise under her right eye where Malcolm's elbow had caught her cheek.

Poppy waited at the bedroom door. "I dreamed last night," she said. "I woke up when the door slammed."

Lena put her skirt in a paper bag.

"Someone was running down the hall," Poppy said. "It sounded like children playing a game." The basket swung in her hand.

"You must have been dreaming." Lena turned so Poppy wouldn't see her flushed face. She powdered her nose and swept the puff up and over her cheekbones.

"There were footsteps right outside my door," Poppy explained. "I nearly got up."

"You must have heard me," Lena said quickly. "I ran down to answer the phone." She put on her earrings and brushed her hair neatly behind her ears. They'd forgotten Poppy was in the spare bedroom. Such a silly business, Malcolm grabbing her skirt like that.

"I'd like it by Friday," Lena said, taking out the skirt. The seamstress draped it over the wedding dress in her lap. "I hope you have time."

Lena glanced down at Poppy who was running her hand over the silky white material of the dress, fingering the seed pearls and sequins. "If it was only the seam I could do it myself."

"Isn't it beautiful?' Poppy placed her small hand flat on the dress and gave a little sigh.

"I don't know." Mary Edwards examined the seam. "It's a nasty tear, right by the zipper." She turned the skirt inside out. "I'll have to pull some threads."

"Do the best you can," Lena took hold of Poppy's hand. "Call me when it's ready."

"Are we going home now?" Poppy asked.

Lena carried the basket filled with groceries while Poppy walked a little ahead. The child's arms and legs were still gangly but she would be a pretty young thing in a few years. Poppy jumped the curb and landed with her two feet on the pavement.

As they reached the front door Lena heard the telephone ringing. She put the basket on the kitchen counter. "Hallo?" she asked.

"Mr. Temple there?" A woman, and young by the sound of her voice. At least this time she hadn't hung up.

"He's at work," Lena said. "I'll give you his number." She could hear the music quite clearly in the background, the syncopation of *Take Five*, Dave Brubeck's famous piece.

Lena began reciting the number but the connection was broken.

Lena called her close friend Caroline. "Can Betsy come over and play with Poppy this afternoon? Norman's walked out again."

"Poppy's staying with you?" Caroline asked.

"She needs to be distracted," Lena said.

Caroline's voice dropped to a whisper. "There's not another woman, is there?"

"Norman always comes back." Lena replied.

"How's your sister coping?"

"She's trying to make things work," Lena said.

"Aren't we all!" Caroline said with a laugh.

Lena and Poppy were finishing a game of *Old Maid* when Betsy arrived. Betsy wore plastic sandals that made an irritating screech every time she turned on the polished boards.

"Can we play in my bedroom?" Poppy asked her aunt.

"Put everything away before Betsy leaves," Lena said, shuffling the cards and replacing them in their box.

Betsy nodded obediently, pursing her little mouth. "Yes, Mrs. Temple."

A short time later Lena came through the hall on her way to the linen closet, her arms full of folded towels. Betsy was standing outside the bedroom door. "I'm just going to the bathroom," the child said, and slipped off.

As Lena put the folded towels on the closet shelves she heard Poppy calling from the bedroom. "You can come home now."

Lena closed her eyes. In that moment, Poppy sounded just like Margaret. She moved the pillowcases and put the clean towels alongside.

"Come on, Betsy," Poppy shouted. "Betsy!" The bedroom door flew open and slammed against the inside wall. Poppy stood in the doorway. Her cheeks were red and her eyes anxious.

"Betsy's just gone to the bathroom," Lena said, patting her shoulder as she walked past.

"I knew that." Poppy's face relaxed. "I knew she wouldn't go without telling me."

On her way through the dining room, Lena picked up the dead frangipani blossoms from the vase on the table. The vase had been a wedding gift from Margaret and was made of fine glass with four graceful arms branching out from the top of a central glass stem. Hooked on the end of each fragile arm was a little glass basket. She went outside to collect the mail and along the warm side wall of the house she picked a handful of violets. Such old-fashioned flowers, symbols of faithfulness. She held them carefully, trimming the stems with her thumbnail to an even length.

The telephone rang as she came inside. "Hallo?" she asked. The syncopated notes of Take Five were clear through the wire. She hung up abruptly. Malcolm would have to make the phone calls go away.

The next day, Malcolm Temple stood before the glass panel in the hall door. "Lena!" he called. "I'm ready to leave." He checked his tie and patted the strip of white handkerchief in his breast pocket.

"Are you going to work, Uncle Malcolm?" Poppy called from the kitchen. She ran out and gave him a swift kiss on the cheek. "Daddy's home, isn't that great?"

"Great!" He gave her a hug and called again. "Lena!"

"I'm here." Every morning they went through the same small routines and she wondered if this was the way marriages hung together, small repetitions, familiar as the ritual of boiling water for tea.

"My buttonhole?" He asked. She realized that his habits were comforting to her. There were none of the theatrical highs and lows that Margaret experienced with Norman, no walking out unexpectedly in the middle of the night. There were other ways to create a little drama and she thought of the shag carpet in the hall and the torn skirt. After all these years, Malcolm could still surprise her.

Lena put her hands in the pockets of her cardigan. "No more frangipanis, Malcolm, the season's over," she said.

He ran his hand down the lapel of his coat as if he had lost something. "Any more of those phone calls?"

"You need to call the company, Malcolm." She said. "I want you to stop this woman from calling."

"Woman?"

"A young woman," Lena said. "She likes Dave Brubeck."

"I'll call the phone company," he said quickly. "Find out what's happening."

"I know you'll deal with it," she said. "You always do." There were some surprises she was not willing to accept.

He was still waiting. "My buttonhole?" he asked again.

"Violets?" she suggested.

"That's a nice change," he replied.

"They won't last long," she said as she positioned the fragile stems in his lapel.

Malcolm kissed her gently on her cheek. "It's sometimes nice to have a change," he said as he opened the door.

Part Three

*"It's not the weight you carry, but how you carry it...
it's all in the way you embrace it, balance it, carry it
when you cannot, and would not, put it down."*

Mary Oliver
from the poem *Heavy*, published in *Thirst*

Severin's Gift

We live alone, Severin and I, at the end of a narrow dirt road some three miles out of town. When we came to our small cottage that first spring four years ago, the dandelions were in full bloom. They were beautiful, an expanse of yellow so bold it hurt to look at them in full sun. Though the cottage was grey from neglect, the profusion of flowers satisfied me immediately; loosestrife had invaded the swampy areas beside the small pond; bulrushes gathered strength on the north side; and wood violets had multiplied near the cluster of white birch. Several old apple trees remained in the long neglected orchard and the meadow stretched beyond the far fence.

Apart from the young fellow who delivers our groceries on Mondays, we don't see anyone for months on end. It suits me, this isolation, and Severin doesn't complain. The city, where her father has made a new life for himself, is off to the east. I left him years ago after a searing divorce and, with Severin in my arms, rode the train to the end of the line searching for a place as far away as possible from him. I left without a backward glance, left the drab grey pavements, the spindly trees, the small plots of smog-dusted marigolds.

Severin was six when I discovered a lumpy area on her upper thigh. Fortunately, it was a benign growth and was promptly removed at the local hospital, a small incision but deep. Her father, though he has chosen not to see us, still feels some responsibility for his daughter and has paid, without question, all the bills for her surgery.

After an overnight in the hospital, Severin came home with only a gauze dressing to protect the sutures. She played outside all afternoon, filling her arms with the loosestrife, standing knee high among the purple-pink spires with the buds unopened along the tips. She planted the flower sprays in neat rows along the edge of the marsh, careful not to wade into the water too far and get the dressing wet. I enjoyed her persistence, the way she moved to and fro as though she was planting a formal garden. She will make gardens anywhere.

A neighbor gave me three bottles of dandelion wine from her cellar as a homecoming present; she is a good soul who watched the cottage while we were away. I drink a glass of the dusty, yellow wine while Severin plays. When she comes over I allow her to sip from my glass. She leans against my shoulder and makes a face before she swallows. The wine has a greenish hue as though the liquid is saturated with life though it might only be the reflection of beech tree leaves through the glass.

When Severin turns seven this September she will go to school. I would much prefer for us to be together and left in peace but the idea of homeschooling is beyond me. She is aware that going to school will bring changes in our lives, will upset the order of things, require alarm clocks and lunch boxes, and farewells. She is reluctant to talk about it, but she knows I will miss her when she goes.

"What will you do?" she asks.

"The day will pass quickly," I assure her. "I'll take care of your gardens."

"I'll leave flowers for you every day," she says, "so you won't be lonely."

Over the next week, Severin's wound heals slowly. My grandmother said that dandelion juice has medicinal properties. She called it *heart's-fever plant* and said it set the good blood pumping into all the hurt places. She rubbed the juice on my cuts and bruises when I was a little girl so it seemed only natural to rub it on Severin's incision.

Severin seems busier than ever as summer draws to a close. She gathers the last of the dandelions, handfuls of bright heads with the white juice dripping through her fingers. She brings her posies into the house and sets them in jars on the table and window ledges and as they dry the silvery spores fly round the room and collect in the corner spider webs.

A week after the dressing is removed Severin raises her skirt. "It's throbbing," she says. The skin of her leg is a warm glowing brown like the good soil in one of her garden beds.

I run the tip of my finger over the scar. "The sutures have to dissolve," I say. There is a very slight weeping at the base of the incision, and three little knobs beneath the skin, each one quite hard under my fingertip.

"It's still healing," I say. "We must be patient."

Severin smiles and brushes my hand away. "I'm glad," she says, lowering her skirt. "It takes a long time, doesn't it?"

"Maybe it should be covered." Severin nods in agreement.

In the evening she takes her bath early for it is very humid. By the time I'm ready to help her in the bathroom she has put on her nightie and placed a fresh dressing on her thigh. Usually I sit on the edge of the bath and splash water over her back, or wash her feet because she forgets to scrub the soles. When she comes from the bathroom, she smells like fresh meadow grass. Her face shines. She goes to bed and while I read in the next room, I listen as she moves restlessly in the hot sheets.

"How is your leg?" I ask in the morning.

"It's good," she replies.

Each day we notice more signs of fall. The loosestrife fades; only its tattered spikes remain ready to slide into the water when the stalks give way. They will grow again next spring, sending up their pale green spears and even though they are considered invasive plants I miss their profusion of bright color against the dark pond. The late summer afternoons cause the trees to cast dark shadows over the water, while the dragonflies zigzag among the cattails their silvery wings catching the last bleak rays of the sun.

"I hate when all the flowers die," Severin says. We are clearing the dead flowers from the garden beds at the front of the house. "I want a garden always."

The lawn has turned brown in patches but the three young apple trees bravely show off their budding fruit. I notice how the waterweed is encroaching further into the swamp, every year taking up more room, while the bulrushes now fill the bulge of water at the northern end of the pond. The dandelions have also spread wildly over the years, advancing further along the bank, growing up to and round the roots of the foremost trees lining the woods.

After supper I see that Severin limps as she returns the empty plates to the sink. "Your foot?" I ask. "Does it hurt?"

She shakes her head. "It's not my foot." She places her sandal squarely on the floor. "See!" she says.

I'm not convinced. Her eyes have a brightness that makes me wonder if she might be running a fever. I sit beside her on the bed after she climbs between the sheets. I haven't checked her dressing in several days.

"Why do you want to look?" she asks.

"To see how it's healing," I reply.

"You won't touch it?" she pushes the sheet down to expose her leg.

"No."

I peel away the gauze. The underside of the white cotton pad is stained a faint greenish color and it takes me a few moments to understand. Out of the end of the incision sprouts three tiny plants, their heads lifting free and upright.

"Do you see?" Severin whispers.

One of the heads, slightly larger than the other two, straightens on its stem, the leaf spikes slowly fan open to reveal its brilliant yellow crown.

Fallen Angels

Beulah Matthews was two weeks old when she was found inside the stone church on High Street. The cleaning crew discovered her one Sunday night wrapped in a pink blanket and cradled in a cardboard box. There was a note pinned to the pink blanket: "Somebody love my baby." So Beulah was adopted by the Matthews, the Reverend and his wife, passed off as their own, and while the elders of the church in Graceville knew the facts of her birth it was kept a secret from the town's children.

Beulah was tall and thin with fine dark hair that blew around her face. She'd twist her hair around her fingers and suck on the ends while she thought on something. Her legs were brown and long and she had the narrowest feet I'd ever seen, though she could run like a rabbit when the boys chased us. My father was a Deacon at the church and my behavior was held to a very high standard but Beulah had a wild, defiant streak, and she singled me out, made me feel important and special. She was my best friend.

"Come on," she'd call to me as I lumbered after her. "Faster, Lizzie!" I'd be sweating from the pace and Beulah would reach her backyard and lean against the toolshed, cool as cool.

The other girls didn't like her. One day, Rosalyn Banks accused Beulah of taking the coins from her purse and rounded on her in the middle of the schoolyard.

"You did!" Rosalyn said, her face flushed, her two best friends standing beside her. "You were the only one in the classroom, Beulah Matthews!"

"Who'd want to steal from you?" Beulah asked.

"You did so." Rosalyn was the center of attention. More children drifted up. "We know she stole." She scanned the group, faced Beulah again. "You steal, that's what you do."

Beulah twisted the ends of her hair and stared at her accuser.

"I'm going to tell Mrs. Brown," Rosalyn continued. Mrs. Brown had strict rules. She zapped our knuckles with the sharp edge of her wooden ruler when we broke them. She taught Sunday school and gave out prizes for good behavior at the end of the year; Rosalyn always received the top prize. "You'll be punished for sure!" Rosalyn said.

"Damn you, Rosalyn Banks!" Beulah spat out the words. "God damn you to hell!" She ran off, and I found her leaning against the outside wall of the toilet, sucking the ends of her hair. "Go away," she called.

"Rosalyn's an awful liar," I said with as much heat as I could muster. I was reeling from the shock of what Beulah had said. "Mrs. Brown's going to be mad at you cursing."

"Just go away, Lizzie, you don't understand anything."

The recess bell sounded and we gathered in the quad. Mrs. Brown stood before us and gave us a lecture on good and evil, the horrors of blasphemy, and the sin of coveting other people's property. Beulah Matthews was called to the top of the steps for the required mouth wash of soapy water. She stood on those steps looking out over everyone's heads, eyes squinted against the sun. She didn't cry, although crying was deemed a necessary ritual for forgiveness. I thought of Joan of Arc and the flames licking up around her legs. She washed out her mouth slowly and spat the sudsy water over the railing onto the dirt, washed and spat. I wondered briefly if she could be enjoying all the attention and blushed at this disloyalty.

On the way home after school, Beulah walked ahead of me and refused to talk until we got to the open field. She threw off her schoolbag and flung herself down on the grass. She rummaged in her skirt pocket, then showed me the coins sitting in her palm.

"You stole them?" So Rosalyn wasn't lying.

"Lizzie," she said. "You're such a funny child."

"Say you didn't steal them," I begged.

"Promise you'll never tell."

"You took them!" Rosalyn had been telling the truth. I gazed at Beulah with new eyes.

"Rosalyn has lots of money," Beulah explained, "and she's so nasty. It's a way of teaching her, you know, like daddy says, something has to happen before you can change, and Rosalyn has to learn that too much money is a sin." She sat up. "I'm just helping her learn that."

"It's still stealing."

"We can put it in the mission box." Beulah's voice sounded lighthearted. Mission box sounded right, an atonement, like the Reverend talked about, though I'd often wondered what happened to the money in the Mission box, if it was really sent overseas, or whether the Reverend used it to buy the watery wine for Communion.

"We can go up to Simpson's and buy a double-header." Beulah giggled. "Come on, Lizzie, we'll say it's your money."

A double-header. I never had enough money to buy a double-header in the middle of the week. "What if we meet Rosalyn? Or Mrs. Brown?"

"We won't." Beulah grabbed up her satchel and we were off to Simpson's little store on the back streets of Graceville. I believed the Reverend when he said money was the root of all evil; my hand trembled so much I could barely hold the cone. Beulah, however, took her time, licking first one side of the cone, then the other, finally making a hole in the bottom so the ice cream trickled onto her tongue. The strawberry in my ice cream had a faint soapy taste.

On the way back, Miss Willy, the town oddity, came round the corner. She was dancing between the sidewalk cracks while the bells on her skirt tinkled. She was upon us before we could run.

"What're you doing back here, my angels?" she asked, voice muffled in the wool of her scarf, her eyes shrewd above the fold of grey material.

"We're going home," Beulah said quick as a flash.

"You hiding out? You don't want to be seen where the darkness rolls over the ocean?" She blocked the footpath. "It's lies, that's what it is, all lies!"

I nearly dropped my cone, thinking she had second-sight. I saw us chained together on the school steps with Rosalyn and her friends throwing stones from below. Miss Willy raised her hands and started to sing,

"Amazing Grace,

How sweet a sound...,"

Beulah ran around one side, I ran to the other.

"...That saved a wretch like meeee..."

When we reached our teens, Beulah began helping in Sunday school classes. She knew how to pray in a special language all her own, a kind of foreign gibberish, and she made me promise not to tell anyone. She'd place her hands on me sometimes when I had a headache, on top of my head, on my forehead, and there was no pressure in her touch. She made those headaches disappear so my head felt light and buzzing for hours after. Sometimes, we'd take something from the corner shop, break a window in an abandoned house, take a shirt from someone's clothesline. "Life is so boring," she'd say, "It's all in good fun." I was tired of the rules my parents set out for me, tired of Sunday sermons, ready to serve my friend.

One Saturday afternoon as we walked down by the Matchem River, Beulah asked if I'd been baptized. Mop Grant and her brother Paulie, were with us. The Grants lived in the house next to mine, and they tagged along whenever we went walking.

"Of course I've been baptized," I said.

Mop and Paulie were throwing stones across the river, making them skip. "Six, seven...," shouted Paulie as his stone bounced over the smooth grey surface of the water.

"I mean as an adult," Beulah continued.

"Once it's done, it's done," I said. We were at the curve of the river where silt collected and the water depth was uneven; a favorite spot for families in the summer.

"This is different," Beulah said. She yelled to Mop and Paulie to come for a special baptism. "Take off your shoes and socks," she said to us, "Follow me!"

They dropped their stones and came running. We all pulled off our shoes and threw them in the grass.

"What do we have to do?" Mop asked.

Beulah walked into the river. This was late spring and the water was warming. She waded in until the water caught at the hem of her dress. I hung back while Mop and Paulie paddled into the water after her. "Come on, Lizzie," she called and I joined them.

"Stand right there!" Beulah pointed to the three of us. "It's a ritual, a proper Christian ritual! Have you been good?" she asked.

Mop covered her face with her hands and bowed her head. Paulie nodded. "We've been good," they said. Paulie splashed water up on Mop's sweater.

"Don't Paulie, this is serious." Mop gave Paulie a little shove.

Beulah dipped her hand in the water and made the sign of the cross on each of their foreheads. "You've been *absolved* from ever sinning again." She slurred the word absolve as if it didn't quite fit her tongue.

"Thank you, Beulah," Mop said politely. Paulie grabbed his sister's sleeve. They headed for the bank, splashing and laughing.

"You've got lots more sins." Beulah said to me. "You've got to come in deeper." She waded out until the water was up to her waist. "Come on, Lizzie. You're a bad influence on me when I'm trying to be good."

She looked as if the top of her body had been severed from her legs and was floating free on the river. "Do you want to be a handmaiden of the Lord like me, Lizzie?"

"Handmaiden?"

"Let me show you," she said and held out her hands. The water was at my chest and my dress ballooned around my body. I could feel the debris, the small stones and slime, the broken tree branches with my bare feet.

She came up beside me, "Close your eyes."

I closed my eyes. She was breathing heavily. I heard the Grant kids yelling from the edge of the river.

Beulah put her hands on my shoulders and pushed down, pushed until I dropped to my knees. My hands scrabbled to touch the river bed. I had forgotten to take a breath. The pressure of her hands was steady. I felt the slime shifting in my hands, touched some discarded cans, grabbed a piece of branch that wouldn't come free. I struggled to find Beulah's leg and when I felt her slim ankle, I pulled with all my strength. She lost her balance. I gasped for air, pushing the hair from my face.

Beulah floated on her back. "Your sins are forgiven, Lizzie!"

"You held me under!" I could feel the points where her thumbs had dug into my skin. "You nearly drowned me!"

"It's all the same in the eyes of the Lord," replied Beulah.

Our friendship ended. I had seen something reckless and mean in her that afternoon at the river. I had become complicit in acts that had begun to scare me. We sat far apart in school, sometimes saw each other on the streets of Graceville but I ignored her. I was ashamed of our former friendship.

One Saturday, I was in Meyers Department Store buying a scarf for my mother's birthday when Beulah tapped my arm. The scarves I was choosing from lay on the counter in a mass of bright colors. The salesgirl had draped a beautiful green paisley scarf over her hair so I could see the effect.

"What are you buying, Lizzie?" Beulah asked. She wore a black dress and no makeup. Her hair was held back with bobby pins so she looked older. She held a small Meyers shopping bag.

I explained what I was doing and she ran her hand through the pile of scarves, sifting them, separating them, fondling the silky softness. From the bottom of the pile she chose a pale creamy scarf with a thin blue border and said, "This one's beautiful." It was as though Beulah was still my best friend. She made me feel worthy of her attention.

The scarf glowed against Beulah's pale skin. I had something richer in mind—the deep green one on the head of the salesgirl or the one with hot pink roses slipping away to the border. My mother had dark hair and thinly arched eyebrows and she wore bright colors most of the time but I bought the cream scarf because Beulah held it to her cheek and said, "This will suit her, Lizzie, your mother will love it."

We waited while the salesgirl wrapped the cream scarf in fancy paper.

"Are you going home now?" Beulah asked.

I nodded.

"I haven't talked to you in ages." Beulah took my arm. "We can walk home together."

We walked arm in arm through the heavy glass doors and there was Miss Willy, singing,

> "...a band of angels coming after me,
> Coming forth to carry me home, swing low...."

Miss Willy beat a tambourine against her hip. Her black hat was tilted on her head. Despite the warm weather, she wore layers of dark clothing and heavy leather boots with scuffed toes. A metal cup containing a few coins lay at her feet. Beulah started to cross the street.

"You shopping girlies?" Miss Willy asked. Her grey wool scarf was wound round her neck with the ends tucked into her belt. "You got change for an old woman?"

Beulah stopped and edged behind me. "Give her some money," she whispered.

I pulled out my purse. Miss Willy smiled at me as I dropped the coins into her cup. "God bless you," she said. "Such a good girl to be caring for an old woman!"

Beulah pulled at my jacket. "Come on, Lizzie," she said.

Miss Willy stepped around me and blocked Beulah's path. "What about you, my angel, what about some Christian giving?"

Beulah's face flushed. "I don't have anything for you!"

"Are you sure, my angel?" Miss Willy reached for the Meyers bag.

Beulah tried to push Miss Willy aside. "Don't touch me! Get away from me!" Miss Willy snatched at the Meyers bag and a length of green silk spilled out at our feet.

I watched Beulah race away, pushing past groups of people on the sidewalk, until the skirt of her dark dress disappeared. Miss Willy's beady bright eyes followed Beulah's flight. She wiped her mouth on her sleeve, "Fat fallen angels!" she yelled. "Fat-arsed angels with flat flying feet!" She shook the tambourine so hard I thought it would shatter.

Beulah changed after Mrs. Matthews died. She was nineteen. She took her mother's place in the front pew and stood in line at the church door beside the Reverend. She read the scripture passages each Sunday, Old and New Testament, and her voice was clear and carried to the far corners of the building. People were moved to tears sometimes, moved to place more money than they had planned into the collection plate.

We couldn't deny the fact that Beulah became a powerful presence in the church. She never missed a service, never missed prayer gatherings or guild meetings. "More," she seemed to breathe, "more and more."

I came home from my first year at Teacher's College and attended the Christmas Eve service with my parents. The church had organized a special service of celebration. The Guild members, my mother included, had collected baskets of food and clothing to be given as gifts to the needy. Tall white candles burned on the altar; the giant wooden cross suspended from the ceiling glowed and the scent of summer flowers was overpowering.

Miss Willy arrived with two other homeless women, Big Lenny who lived by the Matchem River Bridge, and Sally Greeves who lived in a shack alongside Miss Willy down by the railway yards. She walked down the aisle in the midst of the Reverend's sermon, jerking and flapping her arms, calling *Alleluia!* and *Praise the Lord!* in a high, wobbly voice.

The Reverend paused, his hands raised. He motioned them to sit at the back of the church but Miss Willy kept coming until she reached the pew right behind Beulah. She pushed in beside the bank manager and his wife who seemed to shrink inside their clothes. Beulah did not turn her head. Reverend Matthews leaned over the edge of the lectern. His voice soared, "We shall reap the rewards of this night. Blessed are the generous hearts."

When it came time for the hymns, Miss Willy clapped her hands and her body swayed. The voices of the congregation filled the church.

Beulah stood, tall and straight as Aaron's rod, and walked to the small lectern where the bible lay open. Her face shone and her dress glowed in the candle's heat. "Go into the highways and byways and compel people to come…," she read.

She bowed her head over the last words. She seemed to have forgotten where she was as she stared right over the heads of the congregation up to the stained glass window at the back of the church where Jesus knocked on the door of opportunity. Exalted, came to my mind.

She closed the bible and moved to the altar rail. "Miss Willy," she commanded softly. The congregation focused their attention on the old woman. Miss Willy covered her face with her hands.

"Miss Willy!" Beulah called louder. "Come forward!"

The Reverend looked concerned. Whispering rose among the pews. Beulah turned out her palms in a gesture of blessing. "Miss Willy," she commanded again.

Miss Willy limped to the altar rail, her old black hat bobbing, eyes fixed on Beulah. She dropped to her knees. Beulah put her hands on Miss Willy's shoulders and I remembered those same hands pressing down on my shoulders years ago.

Miss Willy began to rock. She groaned and cried, "My angel child, my angel, my sweet angel." Beulah pressed Miss Willy's body down, pressed her face against the wooden floor while we heard the old woman whimper.

"You are filled with wickedness," Beulah cried, and the congregation held its collective breath.

"No!" The Reverend Matthews broke the spell. "No!" he shouted as he came down from the pulpit, his white surplice floating like wings. "Beulah!" he called as he reached her side. He pulled her away from Miss Willy and led her to the back changing-room, holding her up as she stumbled against him. The silence in the church was palpable. Mrs. Edwards, head of the Guild, came down the aisle, flushed and bustling. She genuflected before the altar and pulled Miss Willy to her feet. Everyone waited in their pews as the two women made their awkward, bumping progress to the front door.

And Miss Willy? She still lives in the shanty down by the railroad depot and continues to steal from the street vendors. During the week, she sings with her tambourine and tin cup outside Meyers Department Store. On Sundays, she stands on the uppermost ledge on Vault Mountain with her arms held out like wings and her clothes billowing around her thin legs. She prays for the town up there, prays for her crazy daughter who lives with the

Reverend's sister far away from the good town of Graceville. We know what she does on Sundays because Darcy and Mick Purley spy on her. The boys say if a strong gust of wind caught her full on she'd lift from the ledge and fly.

Oolong Tea

Nellie Anderson walked up the steps and through the door of Hamilton's Antique Shop. The advertisement, neatly typed on thick white paper in the window, asked for "A girl to Tend Shop and Dust Regularly. Apply Within. Marvin Hamilton, Owner."

Nellie was on her way to the train station with redundancy papers from Woolworth's in her hand when she saw the advertisement. She had passed the shop every day going to work, had looked in the dusty windows at the polished silver teaspoons and small Chinese lacquered boxes, the porcelain tea sets and bric-a-brac. When the little brass bell hanging on the door frame dinged, a tall gentleman walked out from the back of the shop. "Yes?" he called.

"You need someone for the shop," Nellie answered. "Mr. Hamilton?"

"Yes." Marvin Hamilton was tall. He was dressed in a dark, three-piece suit, and his mustache and hair were beginning to grey. He was the exact opposite of the young fellow who had interviewed her for the Woolworth's job, a leering boy who stared at her chest.

"I saw your ad in the window." Nellie came further into the shop. "I can start anytime."

Mr. Hamilton waved for her to sit on the smartly upholstered green chair in front of the display case filled with jewelry and thimbles. Nellie sat carefully, knees together, hands in her lap. "I come down on the train each day from Picton," Nellie said. "I can work the hours you're open."

"Good, good!" Mr. Hamilton gazed at her. He brushed his mustache with his fingers, along one side and down the other. It was a handsome mustache. "I need someone to start right away." He had an educated voice, a warm voice. He folded his hands across the buttons of his jacket and crossed his legs.

Nellie nodded. "And the pay?" she asked.

"Above the minimum," he said. "You won't be disappointed, my dear. Your name?"

"Nellie Anderson."

"You can start on Monday," he said with a smile. "I shall draw up the papers and have another set of keys made."

How could she be so lucky? Wait until she told her parents that night, "I lost my Wooly's job today but I have another one that pays better," she'd tell them.

She reached across the counter to shake Mr. Hamilton's hand.

That first week Nellie cleaned the shelf that ran along the two front windows. She piled all the precious china on the floor, the tea sets and vases, the two porcelain table lamps, and scoured the ledge with hot soapy water. She cleaned the windows and dried them with crumpled-up newspapers just as her mother did at home so they shone in the afternoon sun. She was entrusted with the keys to the shop. She was to open and shut the business each day. Nellie liked her new responsibilities.

Those first few weeks, people drifted in, wandered around, asked questions about the price of a piece of furniture, the name of an artist, the date of a painting. She sold the brass table lamp to a lady, the one whose shade was a little worn along the back edge; several little dishes, and three teaspoons to a lady from Melbourne.

Mr. Hamilton came in on Friday afternoon before closing time to collect the money from the till. Nellie liked the way he raised his hat when he greeted her. He was nice and polite, a real old-fashioned gentleman.

"Are you happy?" he asked. "Have you had many customers this week?"

Nellie described the customers who had come into the shop and proudly showed him the list of items sold. Each of the receipts was written out in her small, cramped handwriting.

Mr. Hamilton patted her shoulder. "Very good, my dear, keep it up."

It was restful to sit in the shop. Some days she sat behind the counter and did her nails and read a paperback. The traffic buzzed by in Bourke Street and every now and then a horn sounded. The clock on the Liberty Building struck the hour and half hour and Nellie followed the day this way, counting out the strokes as they occurred, murmuring the hour after the striking had stopped.

"Ah, ten o'clock." She put her book away and went into the little back room. It was hardly a room, more a galley with a metal sink and single hotplate, and a shelf running along the back wall with her packet of tea, tin of sugar, and each week a fresh packet of biscuits. Her mother sent down replacements as they were needed, explaining her long-held belief that, "A cup of good Oolong tea and a chocolate biscuit will change your day, Nellie."

Nellie made morning tea and took it back into the shop. She stood by the front window with the teacup in her hand and watched the people go by. Sometimes pedestrians stopped, looked in the window and, with surprised looks, saw her beyond their own reflection. Once she waved to a young man who hovered outside. He looked as though he'd seen a ghost, stepped back, gave a sheepish grin and walked on, his grey jacket buttoned against the wind.

Nellie drank her tea and washed her cup in the galley sink. She folded the tea towel neatly and went back to her seat behind the counter. Her mother would not have approved of her waving to a complete stranger. "You can never be too careful, Nellie. The city is a dangerous place for young women."

Nellie closed the shop at 4:58 p.m. and caught the Picton train. She found her best friend, Barbara, in the end carriage, but before she could settle into her seat, Barbara grabbed her arm and asked, "Did you hear about the girl in my office?"

"No," Nellie said. "What happened?"

"She was dragged into the bushes in Hyde Park." Barbara held her coat tightly to her chest. "And you know what happened?" Barbara paused. "She was molested." Her voice was hushed, trembling.

Nellie couldn't imagine even saying that word.

"Can you believe it?" Barbara whispered.

"He didn't," Nellie put her hand to her mouth.

"The man apologized and helped her fix her clothes." Barbara explained.

Nellie's eyes widened in disbelief, "A gentleman rapist?" Nellie sighed.

Barbara confided more. The office worker had met the man earlier in a café where all the office girls had their afternoon tea and he was young and seemed polite.

"It was completely unexpected." Barbara concluded.

Nellie stared out the train's window at the passing streetlamps, the blur of house lights.

How could you ever know? Nellie wondered. The only young men who had asked her out were the boys she'd grown up with, and whose parents knew her parents.

"You can't be too careful, my Mum says," Barbara replied.

"But, how do you know?" Nellie rocked with the movement of the train. She raised her legs and admired the glossy leather of her new shoes.

Mr. Hamilton came each Friday and asked about the week: How many people had come into the shop? How much money was taken? He placed his latest small treasures on a length of black velvet on the counter. The furniture he brought through the back door after he had polished the wooden frames and cleaned the upholstery. He brought in a pile of magazines, *Antiques Today*, and showed Nellie what was moving in the market, what people were buying, what he looked for as he went to sales.

"Sit down, Nellie." He gestured to the set of brocade chairs by the window. "I'd like you to study these magazines, begin to recognize the best, learn the names." He flicked through some pages. "Start with the furniture and move on to the porcelain and silver."

Nellie leaned over to see more clearly. She might become a real professional in the antiques' business.

"Yes, Mr. Hamilton. I'll start studying this week. Thank you."

Mr. Hamilton patted her knee. "Quite, my dear." He stood. "Perhaps a little tea now?"

Nellie made some Oolong tea and they sat together in companionable silence, watching the people pass by the window on Bourke Street. She shared her biscuits from a blue Wedgwood dish she fancied.

"I lost my wife to cancer two years ago," he confided. "It's all been very difficult."

Nellie remembered the comforting words her mother had used when their neighbor lost her beloved cocker spaniel. "I'm sorry," she said quietly. "It must have been time for her to go,"

"Thank you, my dear," he patted her knee again. The touch of his hand was warming. She would tell her mother all about his dead wife when she got home that night.

"I do like how you've arranged the jewelry," he said, before he left.

Each week she dusted everything under the glass countertop. She polished the silver rings and bracelets, checking carefully for the maker's identification. She organized the thimbles by size, porcelain in one grouping, silver in another, mother-of-pearl letter openers side by side. Some pieces of jewelry were valuable and Mr. Hamilton had priced them accordingly; others were trinkets and chosen because they added "splash". She enjoyed trying the jewelry on herself, checking to see how she looked in the mirror, the length of the necklace, the size of the stone.

One piece of jewelry caught her eye. An agate ring in a silver filigree setting. The stone was a rich dark red with a silky sheen. Not highly priced but a perfect fit on her ring finger. She took to wearing it in the shop and one night she wore it home.

"You are so lucky," Barbara said when she saw it.

"Mr. Hamilton gave it to me." Nellie held out her hand and the ring glittered. "A little thank you."

The clock on the Liberty Tower chimed ten. She made her morning tea and stood by the front window. The young man in his grey coat stopped on the pavement. He looked in the window and gave a small wave. Nellie waved back. He mouthed "hello" and Nellie couldn't help but smile.

The next day, during the lunch hour, Nellie heard the bell ding. "Hello," someone called.

It was the young man from the street. Nellie put down her *Antiques Today*.

"Can I help you?" She put her finger between the pages. What could he be looking for?

The young man had an untidy mop of hair, a little long over his rather large ears, but his smile was inviting. She noticed his coat sleeves were a little short, his shoes unpolished.

"You come down on the train each day." he said, pointing a stubby finger. "I thought I saw you get on at Picton."

"Really?" She closed the magazine. "You must get on further up the line. Berrima?"

"How'd you guess?" he asked. "My name's Jimmy, Jimmy Buell," he said. "I work in the Liberty Building, city government. I'm learning the business."

"And, I'm learning the antiques business." She slid the magazine across the counter.

Thomas reached over to shake her hand. "Nice to meet you," he said, and Nellie wondered if she was being a little forward with him.

Jimmy had bought a sandwich from the Deli up the street so he and Nellie sat in the two brocade chairs by the window and shared her Oolong tea. They talked about their school experiences only a few years behind them. They compared how they found their present jobs and how they each wanted a dog, though of different breeds.

"I used to work in Woolworth's," Nellie confided.

"Do you like this better?" he asked.

"I like pretty things," she confided. "The pay is better." The lunch hour passed quickly.

On the evening train, Nellie and Barbara talked about Nellie's meeting with Jimmy. Could he be trusted? They discussed the incident with Barbara's office-mate again. The molestation. Had she recovered? Was she still working there?

"It seems a little cheeky, him just walking in off the street like that,"

Barbara said. "Have we ever seen him on the train?"

"Jimmy seems such a nice fellow, surely...."

"Has he asked to meet you after work?" Barbara asked.

"No, no." Nellie flushed at the possibility.

Nellie had been working at the antique shop for three months and liked the two-weekly pay packet, the rush of shopping in the city during a lunch break. Not that the cheque was large but it was nice to see her mother's eyes widen when she emptied a shopping bag on the kitchen table and held up a new dress. Even her dad put down his paper to nod his head.

"You watch your spending," he said. "No shopping at David Jones, now."

Her mother hung the new dress on a pink padded hanger. "Nellie has to think of her future, Sid. She needs to look the part."

Nellie would remember that moment. She had new responsibilities in the antique shop. She had to dress accordingly.

One evening, Barbara greeted her on the train carrying a bag with gold handles. "I had to buy these," she said, pulling a pair of shoes from the tissue paper. "I'm celebrating. I got a raise!" Barbara had been given more responsibility in the Legal Aid office, a larger cheque.

"They're beautiful," said Nellie, admiring the ankle strap, the two inch heels. "Were they very expensive?" Maybe Mr. Hamilton would give her a raise if she learned the value of things, the correct names in the porcelain world. If she spent more time studying the magazines.

"I bought them at David Jones. What do you think?"

"At David Jones," Nellie echoed. She touched the bag and its gold tissue paper. Nellie wanted to buy something there, to carry their bag home with its distinctive logo, its gold-tasseled handles.

"I'll wear them to your birthday party on Saturday." Barbara turned them under the weak light in the carriage ceiling and the silver shoes sparkled in her hand. "This year, Nellie, we leave our teens," Barbara said gaily.

Once a month, Mr. Hamilton moved the shop around. "Customers need to see the items differently," he said, "Afresh!"

He brought in his new finds and instructed Nellie as to their worth and where they had come from. Sometimes he brought a small dish or trinket for Nellie. "A little giftie," he'd say. "A little thank you."

On those occasions he hugged her and Nellie liked the smell of his cologne, a rich musky smell quite unlike the Lifeboy soap her father used. She felt the roughness of his worsted coat against her face. He was strong, and she wondered if he held her longer than was quite proper. But he was a gentleman. Her mother confirmed that fact once Nellie had described him.

On the day of her birthday, Mr. Hamilton arrived with a large bouquet of pink roses. "For you, my dear," he said, placing them on the counter.

Nellie had never received such a large bouquet of flowers, roses; she was thrilled. Mr. Hamilton hugged her and she was uncomfortably aware that she was being held tightly, her cheek pressed against his rough jacket, her back gently rubbed.

"We'll have to find a vase." He released her and reached for a fine glass vase on the mahogany drop-leaf table. He walked to the kitchen galley. "Bring the flowers," he called.

Nellie followed him. He filled the vase with water. "Here," he said. "Arrange the flowers, my dear."

She stripped the paper and gathered the roses at the sink. Mr. Hamilton wrapped his arms around her waist. His hands cupped her breasts. He pressed his body against her back, and the edge of the metal sink pressed into her belly.

"Mr. Hamilton!" She tried to turn but he held her. "Stop! Please stop." His hand reached under her skirt, under the leg of her panties. His breath came in little puffs against her ear. She struggled and he tightened his grip further. Her face smothered in the roses.

"You lovely girl," he whispered. "Lovely, lovely girl." He pulled her panties down and bent her body over the metal edge of the sink. He moved his weight against her back and rocked. "Ah!" he sighed and rocked some more. The buttons of his jacket pressed into her skin through the thin fabric of her blouse.

"My beautiful birthday roses," Nellie thought as her face was pressed further into the petals. She remembered Barbara describing the young man who molested her friend—so friendly, so charming, so horribly unexpected.

At last Mr. Hamilton released her. He helped Nellie pull up her panties, smoothed the back of her dress. "I'm so sorry," he said. "So very, very sorry." He stood in the doorway, his coat still buttoned up. He smoothed his mustache with his free hand and looked thoroughly embarrassed. "It will never happen again," he declared, wringing his hands. "Never!"

Nellie ran to the bathroom. She washed her face with cold water. Was this rape? Molestation? What was she to do? Could she still work here? Could she face Mr. Hamilton again? She looked in the mirror at her flushed face and wondered at her daring. Mr. Hamilton was a gentleman, she and her mother had agreed on that. He kept his shoes buffed to a glossy brown. He had given her the keys to the shop, a huge responsibility.

She tidied her hair and steadied her heart beat. Could she ask for a raise? Barbara was not the only one who could shop at David Jones.

When she returned, Mr. Hamilton had made a steaming pot of Oolong tea. "My dear girl," he said as he placed the tray on the little mahogany table. Side by side on the tray were the precious Meissen cups and saucers she so admired. She reached for a cup and the agate ring on her finger caught the light from the window. How very pretty it looked.

"You will stay and work for me," Mr. Hamilton said softly. "You will stay, won't you Nellie?"

Such a Good Life

"A bumper crop, Marion," her father said as he inspected the peach trees on Sunday morning. "This will do it! Tomorrow we pick." He gave her braid a playful tug.

It was mid-summer, the height of the fruit-picking season and not only were the peaches ready, but the plums, too—Aunt Becky, Santa Rosa, Narrabeen—all of them choice and rounded, ripening on the trees. They were depending on this season, waiting on the luck of the weather, the turn of the winds. The long grey envelopes came from the bank with agonizing regularity; the bank was waiting for a bumper crop, too.

"The skies are clear," her mother said at breakfast, smiling over at her father. "It will be a good season."

"The barometer's holding," her oldest brother said.

"There's no wind," her other brother answered.

"The wind." Her mother sighed. "You'll really pick tomorrow?"

"The men will be here," her father answered quietly.

Her mother ran her hand along the edge of the old kitchen table where the square of tablecloth covered most of the wear. "We'll bring it out from the wall, here." She gestured with her hands.

Marion spread homemade plum jam thickly over her slice of buttered toast.

Her mother had her eye on a new table at Brunley's. She'd taken to visiting the store when they drove in for the weekly grocery shop. "Best maple to be found anywhere," Mr. Brunley pointed at the grain of the wood. "Very nice crafting, very nice. I can see it in your house, Mrs. Hume, yes, I can."

He put his hand on Marion's shoulder. "Wouldn't you like to show off your mother's silverware on this table?" he asked with a broad smile.

Her mother ran her hand over its polished surface and along the beveled edge. "I'm just looking," she'd replied. "Not buying yet."

Through the day they waited but the strength of the wind increased. The clouds rolled across the razorback mountain and that night the rain fell in torrents. No one slept for the rattle of wind and the relentless slice of rain on the single paned windows. The realization that the plums would be pockmarked, the peaches slashed to ribbons, the unripe small fruit dislodged from the branches. More than half the crop would be destroyed!

Monday it rained intermittently, and the dusty ground became a sponge, so waterlogged they couldn't run the tractor; the ladders sank to the second rung with the weight of a man. The black flies swarmed the picker's shirts, buzzed and settled, circled their faces seeking their eyes. They worked whenever the rain let up, clearing the lowest branches, averting their gaze from the fruit left behind. It was heart wrenching for Marion because she knew how they depended on that glorious fruit; everything rested on getting the packed fruit to the Sydney markets.

By Tuesday they knew if the rain didn't clear the fruit would rot on the trees. The fruit already in the shed was packed quickly; the men's hands flying over the bins of graded peaches, selecting for size, packing them layer by layer in the box. When they had packed the grader clean, her brothers tinkered with the machinery, oiled cogs that didn't need oiling, cleaned bins of dried leaves and stems. Marion kept a furtive watch as she glued their distinctive labels on the boxes: E. M. Hume & Sons. The 95 boxes were ready in the doorway that ran the longest side of the big shed, wide enough to take two tractors, two trucks, a thousand cases of fruit stacked squarely. The clouds were heavy and black and building in the west.

The workers arrived to see if there was picking to be done. "No work today!" her father said, and sent them off.

Her father's face looked the way it had four summers ago. Bushfires had come through and taken out the new block of young Aunt Becky peaches; seared the fences round the house. The fire came up the back gully in a roar, smoke and sparks shooting into the air, the eucalypts igniting yards ahead of the main fire line. When Marion walked home from school, the smoke was so thick it smothered the house and the smell was hot and searing.

She heard her father yell, "Is the break holding?"

"That you, Rob?" came out of the smoky darkness. "We're waiting!"

"Dad, it's me." Marion could just make out the shape of her father. The hot smoke burned her throat, scorched her eyes to tears.

If the fire gained intensity, the wet wheat sacks tied to saplings and the buckets of well water would be useless. The men stood along the fences while the women brought hot tea out of the darkened kitchen; everyone was ready to run if the fire jumped the breaks that ran outside the east fence. The whole town seemed to be waiting.

By late afternoon, the air had chilled; the first heavy raindrops began to fall, solid and distinct against the corrugated iron roof. Her father was clearing the long bench of packing paper when he paused, pushed his hat back on his head. Her brothers stopped stacking empty cases. They lifted their heads to the *ratta-tat* on the roof, the sound like newly shucked peas dropping into a metal saucepan. The noise increased as they moved to the doorway, watching into the storm. The ice fell, hard and white and smooth; it bounced on the ground and spat up the soggy dirt.

Her father's shoulders sagged. He cleared his throat, "Time for a cuppa, Marion. Go tell your mother, it's time."

He turned to her brothers, "Nothing we can do here." Her oldest brother continued to stand there, arms folded on his chest. Her younger brother moved slowly to the outside faucet to wash up.

Marion couldn't bring herself to go into the rain. God, hadn't they all worked, pruning, fertilizing, harrowing, day after day, months of preparation. No one understood. Last spring her parents had friends visit and they sat on the front verandah with homemade beer drawn cold from the well. They looked out over the acres of blossom—pink, rose, white blossoms backed by a thick mat of green leaves—they sat and enjoyed the view.

"What a good life you have here," Dr. Channing said, while his wife lit a cigarette.

"The air is so fresh!" Miss Cooke, Marion's favorite teacher, breathed in deeply. "So much beauty!"

Mr. Stebbins, their banker, looked out to the high acre where the nectarine trees were laden with promise. "Must be rewarding to work with your hands," he said.

Marion's father nodded and took a long draft of his beer. Her mother cast him one of those looks of hers, until he caught her looking, then she laughed. "Yes, it's a good life," she said. "When the clingstone peaches are ready I'll give you each a box for canning."

"Marion," her father repeated. "Go tell your mother it's time for a cuppa." She was off through the pelting hailstones, hands protecting her head, tears falling. Her old blue coat would be shorter than ever this winter. Barbara Land had a new coat every season, and took piano lessons with Miss Vickers. She had a paint box twice as large as everyone else's and she had white and red paint. In art class, the people in her pictures looked real while Marion's people looked as though they'd been staked out in the sun for a week. She ran across the yard to the small shed, her gumboots kicking mud over her legs. Now her mother's new table was gone, too, and the unfairness!

She heard the hailstones bouncing off the shed's roof as she ran through the doorway, past the copper washtub that stood on its own stone fireplace, past the farm tools covering the walls and the great slab-built bench where they constructed their first wooden boats and guns.

"How could you let this happen?" Marion wiped her eyes. She didn't know if she was shouting at God or at her father. "How could you let it storm now?" she demanded.

She left the small shed and dashed into the vine-covered pergola where they slung the hammock for a late Sunday nap, where they came in the hot summer evenings to smell the night-flowering clematis. The hail hit the trellis with quick, empty splats and water seeped through the bougainvillea vines on her head.

She came out of the pergola and there was her mother, washing down the back verandah. It didn't seem right to interrupt. Her face was flushed, hair pinned back, the broom flying in her hands. The edge of her mother's skirt was wet and her house-shoes were dark from the splashing water. Her mother flung the bucket of sudsy water up and along the boards until it foamed off the wall and sloshed down the slope to her broom. She swept furiously, gathering the froth to the lip of the verandah and off into the rain, the suds blending with the white of the hailstones on the path.

"Dad says it's time for a cuppa!"

Her mother stopped, and leaned on the broom. "Call them to come," she said breathlessly. Her hands were clasped round the top of the broom handle, as if in prayer but her eyes were open.

That summer when the bushfire was upon them and they thought the house would go, the wind changed direction. Just like that: one moment blowing hard toward the south, the next swinging to the northwest. Jokes that weren't funny brought wild hoots of appreciation and everyone's blackened faces fit the craziness. Her parents hugged each other in full sight of the neighbors; her mother laughed and cried and held her apron over her face, her father put his arm around her mother's shoulders and pulled her to him.

They sat around the kitchen table in silence and drank their tea. Outside the open door the hailstones skittered across the back steps. Marion's father tipped a matchbox on the table top, corner to corner, until their mother took it from him. Then he rolled a cigarette, fingering the tobacco into the flimsy rice paper, running his tongue along the edge. Her brothers stretched out on their chairs and stared at nothing.

Her mother stirred her tea for a long time. Usually she reprimanded them when they did that. "You only need to stir twice," she'd say. "You're not stirring porridge." But no one was going to tease her today. And no one commented on the bucket still standing on the back verandah with the broom propped near it.

"There's work to do in the shed," her father said, pushing back his chair and replacing his hat on the white line of his forehead. Her brothers sprang to their feet.

"You said it was a good crop," her mother's voice was thin and strappy. "You said the hailstorms would miss us this year."

Her father paused halfway to the door. "Go on," he said to the boys, but because Marion was sitting quietly in the corner he didn't notice her. "There was nothing could be done." He took off his hat and held it over his heart. She remembered him doing that last year when he heard Joe Fergussen had died. "That's the way it is," he said. "I wish it was different."

Marion sat in the corner chair and watched as the storm wrinkled the windows and the hailstones exploded on the glass. The silence was awful between her parents. Her mother was intent on pleating the edge of the tablecloth into a fan-shape, the embroidered flowers making snaps of color in the folds.

"I need a new pole for the outside clothesline," her mother said at last, not looking up.

"I'll make a beauty for you." He touched her hand. "With a deep fork this time." He smoothed the neck of her dress where the collar creased up. "You won't have this pole dragging the line over."

"We'll have soup for lunch," she said flatly. "On a wretched day like this, fresh made vegetable soup." Marion wished she would look up. Her father looked odd, unfamiliar, bent over his hat with the white band of his forehead exposed.

A Complicated Case

For two weeks each summer I was sent to stay with my relatives in Sydney. My Uncle Charles was a doctor, a general practitioner in Randwick, and my Aunt Miriam kept the house running smoothly. I slept in a small room off the dining area, what was once a servant's room. My bed ran along a closed-down fireplace and when I woke early I could hear the mourning doves nesting at the top of the chimney.

My uncle liked a boiled egg for breakfast and he mixed the butter and honey to a rich caramel paste before he spread it on his toast. He wore wire-rimmed glasses over sharp blue eyes and his bow tie nestled snugly between the points of his collar; with his black bag in hand he looked every inch a doctor. Uncle Charles taught me to swim and to love opera. I was thrilled by *La Boheme* and poor dying Mimi, and by Tosca with her long, last, drawn-out scream.

"Did Scarpio push her?" I asked my Uncle.

"Of course not," he replied. "Listen more carefully."

Three days a week he allowed me to accompany him on his rounds. On Thursdays, I stayed with my aunt and we sat out on the small balcony that faced the street and sipped green tea and nibbled almond cookies. My Aunt Miriam was pretty. She wore small shoes with bows in front and square little heels. She wore lipstick and powder all day and sometimes she spilled things, especially those days when she shut herself in the master bedroom and told me not to disturb her. "I need a little nap," she'd say gently. "Run off and read a book. It's too hot to do anything else." They had a city bedroom, up a steep flight of stairs to the second floor, to a very large bed covered by a flouncy bedspread. There were curtains on the windows and blinds to pull at night.

"Why?" I asked. "Does uncle sleep in the downstairs room?"

"If there's an emergency in the night, he can leave without disturbing me."

"Every night?"

The pale rug covering my aunt's knees was silky soft compared to the hardy grey blankets on our beds at home.

Aunt Miriam sighed. "Not every night, dear. It's the unexpected he's waiting for."

"Does he get lonely?"

"He's a doctor," Aunt Miriam answered. "He has his books."

That summer it was so hot the grapevine on the outside trellis shriveled up, the green grapes small as peas, leaves drooping. Aunt's old cocker spaniel, Kimmi, got sores down his spine so the fur dropped off his back in clumps. In the long afternoons I'd raid my aunt's cool pantry for peaches and sit under the lower shelf where the extra cooking pots were stacked and let the dry, damp air enter my clothes.

One afternoon I hung over the little balcony and heard the grind of wheels. A boy, balanced on a skateboard, skimmed along the pavement.

He leapt and spun and flipped the board in the air. "Yes!" he called, catching the board as it fell.

I clapped, excited by the boy's cleverness, his red high tops.

"How did you learn to do that?" I leaned further over the little balcony.

"Come down and I'll show you," he called.

My heart stopped for a beat. To try out on a skateboard was beyond my wildest dreams. "I can't," I said. "I'm just visiting."

He stood on the skateboard, pressed back on the lip and flipped the board high in the air. It fell forever, twisting in the summer heat.

Then he was off, sailing over the pavement's cracks.

It was that same afternoon Aunt Miriam fell down the stairs. We had made an apple pie together, with walnuts and cream. I liked working in the kitchen with her. It was the one time she chatted with me, rather than talking at me. I told her about school and mathematics which I loved, how the numbers always stayed the same, while words changed their meaning. We had our lunch of thinly sliced bread and cheese with homemade chutney and when we tidied up my aunt said she'd take a little nap.

Later, I heard her bumping passage and shrill cry. "Help me, child," she called. She had twisted her left ankle so it swelled over her shoe. Tears ran down her cheeks. I felt them on my hands as I supported her to a cane chair.

"Take it off," Aunt Miriam instructed. Her breath smelled. I recognized the smell from old Mrs. Bratten who worked sometimes at the corner store and who mother cautioned us about. I undid the laces and eased the shoe off my aunt's foot while she held tightly to the seat of the chair.

"Get a basin of cold water and some ice. There's a bandage in the top bathroom cabinet." I ran to do as she asked. "And a towel, child."

Later, with her ankle firmly bandaged, Aunt Miriam held my face in her two small hands and said quietly, "We won't tell your uncle about this little episode, dear. It will only worry him."

"But your ankle?" I asked.

"I don't think he'll notice," she said as she limped into the kitchen.

The next day, a Thursday, Aunt Miriam took to her bed.

"Seems you'll be coming with me today," Uncle said as he finished his cup of Bushell's tea. "You have a book to read?" he asked as I climbed into the car. Sometimes I brought two books if I thought I'd finish the one I was reading before we got home.

He drove a large gray Rover car on his rounds. "You need the right car," he told me. "It shows the patient you're successful." The car was wonderfully comfortable after the rock-hard seats of the little Austin truck my dad used on the farm.

He had a list of patients on his lap and a city map on the armrest between us. The houses he visited seemed sad. He strode up and down steps and knocked on dark doors that opened on even darker halls, the black bag swinging in his left hand. Most times he was with a patient for thirty minutes or less. I read *Treasure Island* and *Swiss Family Robinson*, all books my brother had read before me, and the time flew by as I imagined myself into the stories. Then my uncle was in the car and we were driving to another house.

The last stop on his rounds was a rather nice brick house with a red front door and surrounding stone wall. There were birdhouses hanging from the trees, with tiny chimneys and little roosting pegs. The house overlooked the Bondi waterway and I could see a narrow path winding down through lantana-covered dunes to the beach.

"I might be a little longer here," he said, "A rather complicated case." He closed the car door. "Why don't you walk down to the beach and look for shells."

I read for a time and when Uncle didn't appear, I walked down to the beach. The day was gray and the waves came in with monotonous regularity. I collected some shells, nothing worth keeping, but I was there and they would be a record of my visit. A few seagulls drifted on the wind currents and tiny soldier crabs scuttled away from my feet. I kicked sand over them and watched them struggle, imagining myself as Gulliver and the crabs as tiny Lilliputians.

Back at the car, I found the door had locked after I'd closed it. I leaned against the door for a while then I sat against the stone wall in the little shade it provided. I must have nodded off because I felt my uncle shaking my shoulder.

"It's time to leave."

I walked sleepily to the car, the warm sun on my face made everything shimmer slightly so it seemed my uncle's bowtie hung a little askew and his hair looked as though he had just showered.

"You can nap along the way."

He leaned over and clipped my seat belt in place. He smelled different, a sweeter, softer something I didn't recognize. We drove home in silence. The sand had penetrated my sandals and I felt the rub between my toes. When we arrived at the front gate my uncle declared, with the heat, he needed a nap to be ready for house calls that evening.

I found Aunt Miriam on the balcony, a tea tray on the table, her hair drying in large rollers. She had her swollen foot up on a hassock and she was fanning herself. "Did you have a nice time?" she asked.

"I went down to the beach," I said. I put the shells on the table and lined them up, small to large, and the soft interior of the larger shells glistened.

"Very pretty, child." She stopped fanning herself. "Was it near Bondi Beach, a stone house, red door?"

"With birdhouses," I agreed.

Aunt Miriam began taking the rollers out of her hair, piling them in her lap. "He always visits on Thursdays," she said.

The next summer, my Aunt Miriam fell down the stairs of their city house.

"I always knew there'd be an accident," my mother said. "Those stairs were an accident waiting to happen."

"She used to nap up there in the afternoons," I said.

I remembered my last visit when my aunt fell, how awkward I felt when I bandaged her ankle, the weight of her foot in my hands. I couldn't recall if my uncle had noticed my aunt's limp or whether he had rebandaged her ankle after my initial clumsy attempt.

"You can't possibly visit," mother said. "It's all too sad."

I miss those little almond cookies, the pointy bows on her small shoes, the beach where I collected the shells now sitting on my bureau gathering dust. I miss listening to those rather scratchy records of my Uncle's favorite operas and I couldn't quite get it out of my head that perhaps, just perhaps, Scarpio had pushed Tosca off the top of the building.

Cleaning Girls

Mary Franklin started cleaning for me in early February. I told everyone, it's wonderful what another pair of hands can do and we know how hard it is to find a cleaning girl in town. I mean, no one wants to clean houses these days, do they?

Mary came to me word-of-mouth. In our little town of Loriston, that's the way most things are done; you tell Olive at the general store what it is you want, and she's better than a daily newspaper, she gets the word out so fast. The Franklins have only lived in Loriston the past year, but Tommy Franklin has picked up all sorts of jobs; he runs deliveries for Olive at the store, keeps the railway station clean, and plants the flowerbeds and trims the ornamental pines beside the station platform. The flowers are a pleasant sight, and the two tall pines shield the waiting room from the afternoon sun.

Tommy Franklin brought his daughter along to meet me that first day. I opened the door, and they were standing together on the back porch. Tommy had a bright red beret on his head and a protective arm around her shoulders. She was a big girl with a shock of dark hair and heavy lace-up shoes, dusty from walking down the back road.

My, that day when Mary came, was hot. It took all my energy to move from the sofa to the fridge and back with a glass of raspberry cooler. Even the fridge had a hard time keeping pace with the temperature; it was a miracle just getting a decent ice block. The dust seemed to wash through the windows like we were having a storm of some sort; wipe the table, turn away, it was covered again. That's a source of irritation tough to manage on top of prickly heat. All over me it was, chest and back. Didn't know I had so many places I couldn't reach with the Calamine Lotion.

Mary was rather slow. Not that my place is so large, I mean the Masterson's house is larger; being the bank manager you'd expect it. His wife, Jean, is a bundle of energy, though her kids get her down. Not long ago she surprised me at the church meeting by saying, "We need all the faith we can muster to cope with the kids today." I expect she was talking about her own three boys; and Bart, the youngest, as wild as they come.

Mary was an odd one—a nice girl if you like the quiet type, but she had some strange ways. She said in the middle of cleaning out the bath, "I laid out a dead woman once." She wrung out the cloth and looked up at me. "I was only ten," she said.

Of course, at the time, I didn't believe her. A mere child like that wouldn't be allowed near someone who was dead. I mean, the dead person's folk wouldn't let a child near her, would they?

"No," she said. "It really happened."

It bothered me some that she'd told me. I mean if it's the truth then it's something she shouldn't tell, but if it's a lie then she'll suffer. But that day, I was too stunned to ask any more questions, and she went on cleaning like nothing had been said.

She had the whitest, softest hands I'd ever seen—plump and small, wrapped around the handle of the feather duster, pretty hands really. She wore an over-sized pinafore in an ugly floral print to cover her clothes.

I told her, "You don't have to wear a uniform to do the house, Mary, but I expect you to look neat."

"Good enough for my last job," she said abruptly.

I wasn't much taken by her tone, but after that she didn't wear a pinafore to the house again. You've got to instill some pride in these young girls and into the work they do. Most times it's not their mothers who do it anymore. I mean, look around you, how many young people have good manners? Walking into Olive's store the other day young Sydney Green pushes right past me at the door and lets the screen fly back in my face.

I told him off right there in the store. I said, "Didn't your mother teach you any manners?"

He laughed. "Mum left years ago," he said, "and my old man wouldn't know a manner from a left hook!"

I was speechless. Imagine talking to an adult like that.

"Well, what can you expect?" Olive said. "Loriston's going to the dogs with the riff-raff moving into town."

"Makes you ache for the old days," I said as I picked up my groceries.

Mary was cleaning the shelf along the center of the living room wall, and I saw she was putting on weight. I thought she should really be on a diet, but some folks get touchy when you mention weight and such; think you're criticizing them for their eating habits. I put on weight once, had to let out every dress along the side seams, half inch here; an inch there. Hormones it was, but with outfits so expensive, you have to be thrifty. As Mary reached up, the chair seat dipped so I worried for the cane-work, and her feet still in those awful lace-up shoes, square like barges over her toes, and when she stretched to dust I could see the hem of a cheap nylon petticoat.

You'd think Mary would keep her weight down walking into town. There's only one paved road in Loriston and that's the one runs past my house, to the store, and on to the railway station. I feel lucky we bought in the right place, one of the prize locations in Loriston; my late husband, bless him, did right by me. Even the Mastersons couldn't buy in town, they had to buy out on Pinchpocket Road, a mile or so from the Franklin's small place, and Jean Masterson says the dust is terrible.

When Tommy Franklin came to Loriston, he brought Mary and a younger child who died of pneumonia the first winter. She was only a little thing, maybe three years old, with big round eyes and hair that slid down on her face. Always sucking her thumb, but what can you expect without a mother to care for her. Mind you, Mary did a good job looking after her, but she's careless in some ways, and Tommy was always off on some bit of work or other, here and there, though he's ever so careful of Mary.

There was something about Mary that I found, well, disquieting. She'd look at me with those faraway, marble-blue eyes, and I wondered was she listening. One day, I was cleaning out the kitchen cupboards while she was cleaning the stove. It's a dirty job, and I was glad Mary was doing it. My legs aren't what they used to be, and kneeling on the linoleum is more than my bones can bear. It's all right in church; you have those needlework cushions to kneel on.

I said to her, "Mary, make sure the gas is turned off." I didn't like to see her crouching on the floor, head and shoulders halfway in the oven.

"Can't smell nothing," she said, voice muffled.

Anyway, I told her about the church fete and how I was making potholders this year, maybe a few tea cozies. I asked her what she was going to do, because everyone in town does something. It's an exciting event, this annual fete, and the church roof needing money for repairs.

She said, "I'm not good with my hands."

"But, Mary," I said, "everyone has to do their bit."

"No one taught me," she said, "My mum died when I was a baby."

Goodness, Mary surprised me sometimes, stopped my breath she did with the way she put things. I knew her mother was gone, it was the circumstances that continued to nag at me, and where was the mother of the little one. One day I asked Olive did Tommy have a second wife. "Never mentioned her," Olive told me. "When the youngest child died, she was buried without a marker."

Everyone talks about their past in some way, it just drops out while they're talking, a few pointed questions and people are drawn to fill in the gaps. It's neighborly to share those things, makes for less misunderstanding. So Mary's words kept bothering me. I mean it's an unlikely experience for a young girl. Who was it she laid out, and where was Tommy to allow such things.

"Mary," I asked gently, because I didn't want to startle her. "Who was it you attended?"

"Nobody," she said. "I was just talking." She picked up my precious King Henry Toby jug and blew the dust off his hat. My jugs are called Fillpots, such a funny name for pottery figures when you think about it, very English. But King Henry is the most valuable jug in my collection, so I held my breath until she returned it to the shelf.

"Do you want to tell me about it?" I asked, standing behind her.

"No, ma'am," she said, "There's nothing to tell." She dusted each jug in turn, old Falstaff in his green hat and vest, the saintly Lord Gervaise with his meerschaum pipe, the seated workman in his bright red beret, eyes half-closed, all seven of them, she dusted carefully and returned to the shelf.

"But, Mary," I continued, "How come your mother passed away?" I felt badly for questioning her like that, but I couldn't just let the conversation go; I mean, Mary might have a need to talk about it.

"She wasn't right in the head," Mary replied, climbing down from the chair. "She heard voices all the time. And sirens."

Well, I didn't know what to think. There are some things best left alone, though I must say I wasn't satisfied. I wondered why Mary was so removed, so disinterested. Sirens? I tell you, I felt an ache for the girl that morning.

We staggered through another month of heat, everyone complaining about their vegetables and the ground dry as dust. The back tank was low in water, and I called Tommy to bring some extra. He came and filled the tank that afternoon. I filled the bath up to the very top that first evening, and it was a treat—not that I'd do it again; you can't afford to be wasteful. Before he left, he told me that Mary wasn't well.

"Feeling poorly," he said. "She won't be cleaning next Tuesday."

"What's wrong with her?" I asked, thinking of germs and maybe we should start boiling our water before we were all taken with cramps. You get sick, you have to go to Wookera for a doctor, or pay for a house call, which costs a fortune.

"Mary'll be all right," he said, edging off down the path. "Nothing can be done."

Of course I should have guessed. I asked her once what she did for fun, though I knew she had to take care of her father. It's good for a girl to have an odd evening at the movies.

"I stay home," she answered. "Dad doesn't like me going out."

"Well, I'm glad you don't spend time at Larry's Café," I said, thinking she was too young to be going there, yet feeling responsible to ask. Jean

Masterson said Larry's Café should be closed down, his back room filled with pool tables and betting machines, but that was after she heard her son was hanging out there most week nights.

A month it was before Mary came back, and I had a devil of a time keeping the house up to scratch. As soon as she walked in the door I could see how she'd let out her skirt, the tightness of her blouse, buttons pulling. Her hair was like a bird's nest, and she wouldn't look clear into my eyes, just muttered hallo and went straight to the cleaning cupboard for the duster. She didn't do as much as usual, and I found I was running around behind her, helping and dithering, not able to feel comfortable enough to talk about her condition. I mean, what should a person say?

I didn't really need any groceries that afternoon, but I decided to check if Olive had some fresh tomatoes, not that they're good for me, acid plays havoc with my arthritis, but they're a nice sight in a lettuce salad. And Olive said everyone was talking.

"Jean Masterson was in yesterday, and she's not at all happy," Olive said. "There's talk about her youngest boy."

Well, Olive's always been outspoken. She knows the town better than I do, so I wasn't going to deny what she said, but I couldn't quite see the connection. Jean's boy ran with a different crowd of young people, and Mary was so dull by comparison.

The following Tuesday, Mary came to clean. Her mind wasn't on her work. She moved from room to room heavily, pushing the vacuum cleaner over the carpet, not thinking to move the furniture. She wiped off the stove and started cleaning the sink.

"Use the new cleaner I got at the Wookera hardware store," I said to her. "Works wonders on the porcelain."

"How do you go up there?" she asked. I wondered that she didn't know about the new bus that comes from Wookera twice-weekly, a day's trip and plenty of time for shopping. I don't drive anymore, so the bus is a godsend.

"I've wanted to go to Wookera," says Mary, "Some things you can't buy here in plain sight of everyone."

I should have known. Late on Monday afternoon, Mary was found. The oldest Masterson boy went looking for Tommy to do some paint work on their picket fence. Of course he cut her down before he did anything else. It took a deal of time with only a penknife, and the rope so new and strong. He could see it was too late to get the doctor so he drove back down to the store and told Olive, and she did what had to be done. Olive said later how terrible it was for Tommy when he got there, just went to pieces he did, and the Masterson boy having to pull him away from Mary's body.

It's always easy in hindsight to see where things were leading. I realized why Mary hadn't bought the rope in Wookera. Olive's sharp as a pistol, she would have guessed something was afoot. Makes me sad just thinking of Mary again, and what she was planning all the time she was cleaning my new sink. Not a word from her, nothing to alert me.

Mary was buried in the same cemetery plot as her little sister, and most everyone came to the funeral. Tommy sat slumped in the front pew and went through the ceremony like he was sleepwalking. The funeral was on Saturday, and on Sunday he packed up the house and left; didn't even lock the door. The odd thing was he took the time to cut down the two pines outside the railway station; it doesn't look the same with those two pines gone and sawdust spread around the stumps. No one's bothered to take the trees away, and they're still laying there, one on top of the other, the way they fell.

I miss Mary. The new girl who does for me isn't as good; she's seventeen, and a little wisp of a thing who doesn't know one end of the feather duster from the other. She needs a lot of training and talks all the time, too, gossips away as she stretches up to dust the shelf where I keep my collection of lovely Toby jugs. All seven jugs are lined up the way Mary had arranged them, fat Falstaff, Lord Gervaise, and the others, with the smiling workman in his bright red beret at the head of the set.

Uncle Lawrence

Lawrence was my mother's brother. He had been a frequent guest at our house in London, dining with us on Friday nights when father worked late, bringing small exotic gifts in his coat pocket for each of us in turn. I was interested in rocks then, and I remember the feeling of excitement and pleasure when he brought a parcel for me—a rock from Stonehenge, a glittering piece of malachite.

One night, he produced a single pearl for mother. It was balanced in a silver half shell and he said that the pearl reminded him of the Botticelli painting. I was too young to understand the reference then, but I noticed mother's flush as she turned her face away and Uncle Lawrence leaned over to kiss her cheek. Peta and I were sent from the table as soon as we finished dessert that evening and on the stairs we heard their laughter.

On those Fridays when Lawrence came to dinner, mother took us to meet him in Milton Park. My sister, Peta, came with us in a high-set pram with huge wheels and a great dark hood. Mother was beautiful and the policeman held back the traffic with his white gloved hand when we appeared. We met Lawrence by the central fountain, where the water splashed up and over a series of leaping dolphins, around the rim of the fountain were smaller dolphins spewing water back into the pool. Lawrence came from the underground station on the west side of the park and when he came into view, mother left us and walked toward him. Sitting by the fountain, waiting for them, I covered the hole in the dolphin's mouth to damn up the water but my hand was small and I didn't have the strength to stop the force of that water.

"Hallo, Nigel," Uncle said, always with the same surprised lift to his voice as he reached me, before he placed his hand on my shoulder. We walked back along a quiet path he showed us on our first meeting, a path bordered by flaming azaleas rich with shadows. Every few yards or so stone statues were set among the sprawling lower branches of the shrubs.

Lawrence pointed them out with his umbrella. "Those are the pretty gargoyles."

One day I asked Lawrence why the statues were there. "Those are the watchers," he said, putting his arm round my mother's shoulders.

The gargoyles scared me. They grinned malevolently from among the leaves, their hard grey stone splattered with bird droppings so I held the side of the pram tightly and concentrated on not catching the end of my jacket in the wheels. Lawrence picked blossoms from the azaleas, a slate-pink one for mother, a bright crimson one for Peta. Mother tucked her flower into the tortoiseshell clip in the side of her hair and Peta spent the rest of the walk trying to balance the flower on top of her head while the petals fell away on her blanket.

Sometimes I adopted a pose of Uncle's, or mimicked a phrase of his, and mother would smile slightly and say to my delight, "Goodness, Nigel, you remind me of Lawrence when you do that." But then, more often than not if I was standing close to her, she'd gently push me aside.

He was very handsome, tall and smooth-skinned and he was funny, or that's what mother said. "Lawrence is so amusing," she often said to father. "He makes me see things differently."

"Eh? Differently?" Father was a serious man who dealt with the world and its oddities in a myopic fashion, from behind his briefcase or business magazine, his gold-rimmed glasses fitting the red indentation on his nose.

"Yes," Mother said, and there was something vaguely rebellious in her tone. "We're going to see Margot's exhibit at the new gallery tomorrow, her new watercolors."

"Really, Claire, Margot Leacock can't tell the difference between a Picasso and a Henry Moore." His newspaper rustled. "She's not still doing horses, is she?"

Mother ignored him. "I can't imagine what it will be like in Brisbane," she said fretfully. "There won't be a decent gallery anywhere."

"It's only for two years after all," he replied.

My father had received an unexpected promotion to a sister-company in Australia and mother was busy making all the arrangements for the change. When Lawrence came to see us off at Heathrow Airport, he carried mother's bags and held her arm while father stood in line waiting to clear our tickets. When father was done, mother sent him off on one errand after another. I trailed after him, pushing Peta in her stroller while he gathered snacks and magazines, drinks and butterscotch. We boarded at last and the plane rolled away from the loading area. I glimpsed Uncle Lawrence in his dark suit waving to us behind the great glass windows.

We arrived in Brisbane and were overwhelmed by the lushness, the abundance of colors, the midday heat, and the late afternoon thunderstorms when the air cleared into a hazy, humid dampness. I adjusted to the cheeky freedoms of the small local school where the children poked fun at my accent and held their noses to produce a high nasal whine, "Little Nigel wants to blow his nose," they chanted.

Every Monday, a bulky airmail envelope arrived from England packed with sheets of rice paper covered in Lawrence's scratchy black handwriting. "He worked in ciphers during the war," mother said when I commented on his writing. "He was very good."

She read his letters avidly, every now and again lifting her head to stare out the window with a wistful expression; sometimes she laughed joyfully and placed her hand over her mouth to stifle the sound.

"I can't understand Lawrence," father said. "I often wonder how you two survived that family of yours." And turning to me would say, "Your grandparents were quite mad, Nigel, as only artists can be."

It was about this time that Lawrence sent a porcelain vase to mother. When she saw it, she held it against her sweater and said, "Dear Lawrence. No one must touch this." She placed the vase on the window ledge in the living room where the sun comes through the poinciana leaves in the late morning and the pale yellow glaze of the vase changes to an iridescent sheen.

Father saw it that night. "A new vase?" he asked as he picked it up and ran his hand over the surface. "Beautiful," he said

Mother turned the page of her book and I waited for her to explain, but she said, "Yes, it came from London," in an off-handed way.

"It looks like something Lawrence might send." He said and put the vase back carefully on the ledge.

I asked once why father didn't like Lawrence. "He's never really understood him, that's all. We were different, Lawrence and I." She shrugged her lovely shoulders. "It was expected of us, with a portrait painter and a cellist for parents. They were so busy, never home...." She gathered up the belt of her dress and wound it round her fingers. "Lawrence and I did everything together."

Lawrence came to Brisbane when the poinciana trees balanced their flowers like red Christmas candles on the tips of their branches. "He only has three days before he goes on to Hong Kong," his mother said. "We have so much to catch up on, so many things to share."

Uncle's visit had coincided with my father's week-long conference in Switzerland so father postponed his own travel plans for twenty-four hours. He went to fetch Lawrence from the airport and when they arrived home father carried the two bags into the hallway with a great deal of noise and chatter which was unusual for him. Lawrence had the crumpled look that travelers have; his shirt collar was creased into his neck and his skin had a pasty shine. His eyes were the same pale grey as my mother's and they sought out hers while father rushed off for glasses and ice.

We, Peta and I, had been given an early supper and immediately after greeting Lawrence were sent off to bed. Mother tucked us in with our favorite books but Peta complained from her small bedroom across the hall that she wanted to stay up with Uncle Lawrence and I felt slighted in having to join Peta this way.

"He is exhausted," she said, kissing me on the forehead. "And we have to spend time with your father before he leaves."

Father left on his trip early the next morning, and mother made a special breakfast of blueberry pancakes for Peta and me while Lawrence remained asleep in the guest room. She packed us off to school with a reminder we could spend time with him when we got home.

I had forgotten about my Boy Scouts meeting that day so on the first afternoon of Lawrence's visit I arrived home late, just before supper. I went straight to the patio where I could hear their laughter. Mother sat with her head tipped to the side, her hair loose and bunched up as she cradled her cheek in her hand. Three lighted candles were arranged around the yellow vase; a purple iris leaned from its lip. Lawrence was bending forward, speaking earnestly. His face was flushed; his shirt was unbuttoned so I saw for the first time the heavy gold chain round his neck. Until then, I had never seen him in anything but a three-piece suit, carrying a furled umbrella.

Lawrence straightened in his chair as I came along the patio. "Home at last!" he said. He stood and extended his hand as though he hadn't met me before. Mother drank from her wine glass. "He's very like Charles, isn't he?" Lawrence said to her.

Peta came up from the garden with a bouquet of yellow daisies. She went to place them in the vase with its single iris. Mother stopped her. "Find another vase and put them in the guest room," she said. Peta's eyes filled with tears. Mother pushed back her chair, "Both of you go up and wash for supper." I followed Peta and I thought I heard Lawrence say softly, "Little gargoyles."

Peta grumbled about mother getting to be a sourpuss, and why was she so unkind with Uncle Lawrence there. Peta had told me on the way to school that morning she thought Lawrence was the most handsome man she'd ever known. She'd looked at me and said petulantly, "I wish you were more like Uncle Lawrence."

She was right. I was very like my father then; he was a slight man but wiry and proud of his energy. I had been lifting weights regularly that past year, twenty-five times each night, hoping to raise some muscle. I had my father's fair skin, too, while Lawrence had wonderful olive skin like mother's and Peta's, skin that tanned as soon as the sun rose on it.

While we had supper, Lawrence talked of his last trip to Paris. "Did you hear that, Nigel? Your uncle was at Timothy Close's opening in Paris. I remember when he was still trying to paint with oils, and now look, he's made a name in acrylics." I was captivated by their stories and the pleasure in mother's voice as she told them.

Peta asked me on the way to school the next morning if I thought Uncle might stay longer. "Might he?" she asked. "If we asked him kindly."

"He won't," I said.

"Why not?" asked Peta.

"Father will be home on Thursday."

That evening mother prepared supper for Peta and me and made my favorite dessert, a strawberry trifle with whipped cream. She and Lawrence were going out for dinner, and we were to put ourselves to bed. "Your uncle wants to see Brisbane's night-life," she said as they left. "We'll have dinner in town."

It was very late when their car drove in and the garage door rattled shut. The porch lights shone through my window all night, and I was bothered, because my father was particular about the porch lights, about not leaving them on, not wasting electricity.

On the last afternoon of Lawrence's visit I came home from school and bounded into the kitchen. There was always a tin of home-baked biscuits to eat and a jug of cold milk in the fridge. I slid the schoolbag off my shoulders. Lawrence was embracing my mother, his arms low on her waist, her head nestled into his neck. The tray set for their afternoon tea, all silver and porcelain, lay ready on the table. They broke apart as my bag hit the floor.

"Nigel," mother said. "Do knock before you enter a room."

Dinner was a strained affair. I sat in father's place at the table and mother didn't notice. She was preoccupied and Uncle Lawrence filled the awkward silence by asking me rapid-fire questions about school. When my attempts at conversation failed, he teased Peta, and Peta enjoyed the attention until mother broke in on Peta's spate of gossip. She touched my arm and told Lawrence I was interested in lifting weights.

"You lift weights?" he asked in surprise. "Why, I did that when I was about your age."

"There's a lot of arm wrestling at school this year," I answered. "I'm building up for competition."

"Arm wrestling?" Lawrence said. "You must show me how good you are when we finish dinner."

Peta cleared the table and mother served coffee. "Uncle Lawrence is very strong," mother said to me. She laid her hand on her brother's wrist. "You remember poor Tommy? At Winchendon."

"He wore an excruciating green coat with wide lapels," Laurence smiled. "He thought you were marvelous."

Mother laughed. "Lawrence," she said, lowering her voice. "Tommy was only trying to be friendly."

"He played a terrible game of tennis."

"He never spoke to me again." Mother gathered her hair up and made a loose knot of it on top of her head. The soft mass of hair held momentarily before it tumbled down in a golden wave.

"Let's get on with it, Nigel," Lawrence said brusquely.

I rolled up my sleeve. I needed to bare my arm, the freckled whiteness of my skin. Lawrence finished his coffee; even Peta was quiet for once. We sat across from each other at the corner of the table and he pushed aside the cloth and rested his elbow on the wood. We clasped hands. His arm was longer than mine. The pressure of his hand was steady and it took all my strength to hold it there, upright between us. He was watching me. The muscles in my arm and shoulder gathered pain. I could feel the tremor of tiredness and my wrist was close to breaking. I didn't want to see his expression, or for him to see mine.

He pushed. One hard sustained jolt of pressure. My fingers were squeezed relentlessly; my hand rocked. My knuckles cracked as they hit the table top. I heard Peta move in her chair.

"Good show!" Lawrence said, and looked over at mother.

Mother rose from the table and stacked the coffee cups on the tray she had left on the sideboard. Her back was to me. I stood behind her, blocking Lawrence off with my back until she turned and looked at me. Her eyes were unusually bright. "That's enough for tonight, Nigel."

Peta began to protest.

"I'm tired," mother added. "Lawrence must leave early tomorrow morning." She glanced at him. "You'll be in Hong Kong this time tomorrow night, won't you?"

"Yes," he said, his voice was withdrawn.

I ignored Lawrence and continued to stand in front of mother as Peta drifted sullenly to the door. Mother kissed the top of my head. Her hair brushed my face and I smelled its perfume.

"Say good-bye to Uncle Lawrence," she said quietly, but Peta and I reached the door together and neither of us looked back.

We didn't return to England at the end of those two years. Mother never forgave father for his decision to keep us in Australia. Eight years have elapsed since Lawrence visited us, and every year mother has spent a month in London with her friends. And though she rarely mentions Lawrence, we understand she has seen him.

Then, a month ago Tuesday, Lawrence died of a heart attack. He was alone at his office in the London shop, working late on some catalogues. His business partner opened the shop in the morning and found him. His partner, Edward Lacey, phoned mother with the news.

She in turn telephoned me at my apartment. "Lawrence has died," she said. "I'm going to London tonight. I haven't told your father. Nigel, please don't let him follow me."

I had a hard time convincing father to stay. "She's with her friends," I said. "She'll only be gone a week or so. You know how close she was to Lawrence." On and on I reasoned with him and I wondered why it had become important to me that mother should have this time alone.

Father was puzzled. "I can't understand her rushing off like this. I'd have gladly gone with her."

He was away on one of his business trips when mother returned, so it was I who picked her up at the airport. When I saw her I knew some part of mother had died in London. She shut herself away in the spare room, sleeping there, having her meals on the small table with the pale-yellow vase Lawrence had given her. She motioned us to leave when we tried to gain her attention. She sorted through the letters Lawrence had sent through the years, bundles of airmail paper tied in black velvet ribbons according to the year.

One afternoon I heard father trying to reason with her, to break through the terrible cycle of grief in which she had bound herself. He came down the stairs, shaking his head, "She has gone from me," he said.

Peta and I have shared in looking after mother since her return. As a computer consultant my hours are flexible so I spend the mornings at home in case she requires anything, and Peta is there in the afternoons. My sister, at eighteen, has become a fine musician, a flautist in the city orchestra.

Father spends more time overseas now than he does at home. "I doubt she will miss me," he said when he accepted his new position with the firm and I secretly agreed.

Peta and I have our evening meals together before I leave for my apartment, and we lower our voices, for no good reason; mother can't hear us and father is never around. We enjoy similar small pleasures—a book, a movie on TV—and we seem to find humor in the same situations. Once she told me a story of a fellow musician, a violinist, who had been asking her for a dinner date. She laid her hand on my arm and laughed. "He's such a prig, Nigel, such an awful prig!"

I hadn't realized how close we had become until last evening. She went off to a party with her friends from the orchestra and I stayed with mother. She dressed in a gown, a rusty-red one, the color of poinciana blossom, and the hours closed in on me. I bullied mother into playing a game of cards but she was forgetful and bothered by my presence. Finally, I sat downstairs with an open book, waiting for Peta's return.

When at last she arrived, she was full of her friends' stories and we had a cup of cocoa while she recounted every small event and I enjoyed her laughter, her eye for detail. It was late when we parted. I waited inside the front door to switch off the porch lights. I watched as she swept up the stairs, holding her long dress above the steps so she wouldn't trip. I waved to her as she turned on the landing and she blew me a goodnight kiss, just a touch of fingertips to lips.

I imagined the soft sigh of the door's closing. We were children again, Peta and I. It was around the time of Uncle's visit, and I had burst into the upstairs bathroom thinking it was empty. Peta was there. She was sitting on the edge of the bath, wiping between her toes with the end of the towel, her knee cocked to her chin. She was outlined against the window where the asparagus fern, hanging from the window frame, trailed down behind her back and the light slicing through the fronds on her bare shoulders dappled her skin.

"Nigel," she had said in her small girl's voice. "You need to knock before you come in."

Free Flight

Alice Hedley stared into the sky, eyes shaded against the sun. We were standing in Jean Watson's garden at a luncheon for faculty wives and I stood quietly beside her as she watched the hawk hold itself high and free on a wind current. "How can a bird stay so still without ever falling?" Alice asked me. Her long oval face and white neck reminded me of a woman in one of Modigliani's portraits, except for her hair, a thick mass of unruly auburn curls that overwhelmed her face.

"It's a chicken hawk," I told her. "When it finds its prey, it will dive."

Alice turned. Her eyes were grey with a greenish ring around each iris. "Time passes so slowly here. I'm thinking of landscaping the back yard, putting in a sundial just to keep track of it." Alice and her husband, Thom, had come from New Zealand several months earlier when he accepted the position of principal at the newly-built Montrose Academy. It was a job my husband had applied for and failed to win.

"I can't imagine finding time for such a large project." I thought of our untidy back yard where the blackberry vines had upended the fence. "Neil Johnson lives close by. I'll give you his number." I had wanted Neil to clear the vines and stabilize the fence for months but he was always booked.

"You have your boys, Kate. And David's steady as a rock, isn't he?" She turned back to watch the bird. Her hair was tawny-red in the sunlight.

I watched the bird float on the wind currents while bursts of laughter and conversation came through the open window. My friend, Jean, had planned the luncheon to bring together those women whose husbands taught at Warwick, the old public school, and those from the more prestigious Montrose Academy. "We have to bury the hatchet," Jean said, when she called me about it. The building of Montrose this past year had come as a shock to everyone. Several teachers from Warwick had been hired at the Academy and their wives were careful to dismiss their good fortune and better pay. The Hedleys had arrived with money enough for a stylish two-story modern house on the street behind ours with a rose garden in front and a line of jacaranda trees along the back fence.

As I continued to watch the hawk, it suddenly disappeared over the horizon. How would it feel to be untethered? Weightless? I was content with the life David and I had created, the rush of caring for three teenage boys in a house too small for our family. But there were days when I felt smothered.

"I always wanted to have children," Kate said, "But Thom says we have enough kids in our lives." She took my arm. "I guess we'd better go inside before they wonder where we are."

"It's funny," I said to David after supper when the boys were finally in bed, one of those days when I was ready to sell them off to the lowest bidder. "I saw Alice Hedley today at Jean's. She was staring at a hawk."

David put down his book, his forefinger between the pages. "A hawk? Jean has birds now?" His foot tapped in its leather loafer.

"In the sky," I said. "Alice was standing out on the lawn, watching a hawk in the sky. She wanted to know how long it could hang there." I turned the leg of Sam's jeans inside-out and began stitching the seam. Sam was eleven, our rambunctious youngest.

"So?" he asked. He stared at me over his glasses.

"So? It was odd somehow. Everyone inside chattering their heads off and there she was in the garden." I threaded the needle again. "She told me she wanted to have children."

"You were in the garden, too." Sometimes David misses the larger point. I tell my friends that trying to make David understand me has made me a patient woman.

"You know how claustrophobic those mornings are, everyone topping everyone else's stories." I pointed the scissors at David's chest. "I just couldn't sit through another money-saving recipe." I cut the thread on Sam's jeans, found a button to sew on Jamie's shirt, and picked up Phillip's pajama coat where the sleeve was ripped at the armhole. Phillip was sixteen and our oldest. "No," I said to David. "I wanted to see the new day lilies Jean had planted."

"Alice was watching a hawk?" David asked, as if that was the point.

"She was standing by the crabapple tree totally absorbed." I stopped sewing and put the pajama top down in my lap. I couldn't imagine Alice picking up a mess of toys, let alone mending a ripped pair of pajamas.

I passed Alice often—at the shops on High Street or when I walked the dog and we met on the side roads. She was always dressed so smartly, so freshly ironed, so completely the principal's wife.

"Are you settling in?" I asked when we first met. "Is Thom glad to be at Melrose?"

"The boxes are unpacked." She waved a brown paper bag that rattled metallically. "And I'm planning the garden."

As I looked puzzled she pulled out a trowel and laughed.

"You found Neil?" I asked.

"He's just what I needed." Alice said, swinging the paper bag at her side.

Some weeks later I thinned out my garden beds and thought Alice might be pleased to have a few extra violet plants, some cuttings of vinca. I called out as I came to where the wall stretched in a broad semi-circle facing away from their house, and walked down the five steps to where she was working. I was surprised at what she had done. Two large flat stones lay waiting to be inserted as seats and I could see the hollow spaces where flower beds would eventually be set. Off to the side was an elaborately designed sundial resting on a block of stone, as the sun caught the metal pointer it cast a pencil-thin shadow on the brass plate.

Alice was wearing heavy gloves and a large straw hat covered her hair. She was on her knees before a pile of slate, handing pieces to Neil Johnson. I heard Neil's voice coming in snatches as he set stones in place, adjusting and discarding as needed. The wall was as high as his waist.

I called to Alice and she waved. "Glad to see you," she called gaily. "Look how much we've done." She looked more animated, more radiant, than usual.

"It's looking good, Mrs. Wade, isn't it?" Neil grinned at me. "Should be finished by the end of summer!" He was in a T-shirt with the sleeves rolled up, his arms shiny with sweat.

"It's so private," I said to Alice.

Neil and Alice exchanged smiles. "Alice says it's perfect," Neil said.

I placed the newspaper package down on a pile of slate, "Some cuttings for the new garden," I said. Violets and vinca. I wondered if these simple plants would find a place in this elaborate construction.

Alice rose and brushed off her jeans. "That's so thoughtful," she said. "Come up to the house and have a cool drink." She turned to Neil. "Take a break and we'll finish the work this afternoon."

"Okay." He stretched his arms over his head.

We had some lemonade in the kitchen where a fresh bowl of flowers was centered on the cleared table top. Alice described what else she wanted done before the grotto was completed. *Grotto* had such a romantic connotation. "I'll set the sundial in the center, have more topsoil brought in, plant annuals around it."

"Maybe this will inspire David," I said. "Between soccer and the dog, I can't think when he'd find time though." I put my glass in the empty sink. "Does Thom help?"

"He's not interested. Montrose has become a monster. All work for him."

It occurred to me how hard it must be, to move to a new community, and have a husband consumed by his work. "Are you happy here, Alice?"

"Happy?" she stopped rinsing the glass in her hands. "I'm working on it." She shrugged.

David and I threw a party in March and invited the Hedleys. I was putting out another plate of hot pastries when I saw Alice talking to Phillip. He was wearing the new blue Oxford I'd bought him, looking more like David every day. Alice laughed and it seemed louder because of the sudden lull in conversation. Thom looked over at her. She patted Phillip's arm and Thom gazed after her as she moved to join a group by the window.

The Hedley's left late in the evening when our few remaining close friends took their leave. I had noticed they had stayed apart from each other, Alice on one side of the room in her stylish black dress, Thom on the other. She appeared to ignore him the few times he moved close, but she seemed to enjoy the company of our friends. I gathered the jackets and wraps from the bedroom and David helped Alice with hers. I saw him adjust it on her shoulders and simply lift her hair out from under the collar. It was an unusual gesture for him, oddly intimate.

While we were preparing for bed, David said very little. Usually we exchanged bits of gossip, laughed at the idiosyncrasies of our friends, commented on how the food had worked, whether we'd had enough whiskey. Tonight we were awkward with each other as though we'd argued about something important.

"Her hair is glorious," I said. "What did it feel like?"

"Weightless." He threw his clothes in a pile on the floor. Why did he always do that when he could easily toss them in the clothes basket? He didn't ask who I was talking about.

"Is that all?"

"Don't be silly, Kate, of course that's all." He pulled on his pajama pants.

"Do you think everything's okay between Alice and Thom," I asked.

David picked up his book and climbed into bed beside me. "Come on Kate, leave Alice for Thom to figure out."

I only saw Alice in passing and, yes, she said, the garden was emerging. Easter was a busy school holiday with David's sister and her family coming for a few days and my parents joining us, too.

In mid-May Thom phoned to invite us for dinner.

The vase in the center of the table was overflowing with fresh flowers and the silverware gleamed on the white tablecloth. Thom spent a great deal of time decanting the wine. He had a fancy device to pull the cork and he wrapped a white serviette around the bottle before he poured the wine into a silver jug. David laughed a little more heartily than usual and I realized he found Thom's artifice unsettling.

Our conversation finally settled upon our shared interests—the schools, the small town gossip, how to build stone walls that wouldn't collapse in the first heavy rains. Thom was collecting Australian reds to fill his new wine cellar. David was planning fresh ways for kids to carry out his environmental project this year. While they talked, Alice invited me to see what she'd accomplished with Neil.

"Going to the garden again?" Thom asked in his rather prim voice. "This project has taken over our lives," he poured more wine for David.

"I need to show Kate the flowers," Alice replied.

She turned on the outside light and I followed her down the paving stones to where the back lawn dipped five steps down to the lower level. This wall was no amateur effort. It enclosed the space and made a small amphitheater. The sundial had been placed in the center circle and two ground lights, set on either side, shone on the brass plate.

"It's beautiful!" I said, sitting on the warm stone seat. "I had no idea you had done so much."

"I've really worked." Alice stood by the sundial and ran her fingers over the Roman numerals. Along the fence the blossoms on the jacaranda trees looked like small purple moths caught in the branches.

"I'm pregnant, Kate." Alice flattened her hand against the front of her dark dress.

"That's marvelous, Alice, congratulations!"

"Thom doesn't know yet," she glanced at the open window of the living room. "It's not his."

"What are you saying, Alice?"

"Neil starts at Langley Tech next month, landscaping classes," Alice continued. "Thom helped him enroll."

The jacaranda trees were close and overpowering. "Neil's gone?"

"The garden was the only way, Kate." She ran her hand down the sundial's metal pointer. "Do you understand?"

I stood and brushed off my skirt. The stone seat was cold and hard.

Alice came close and linked her arm in mine as though we were co-conspirators.

"Neil will be away for two years or more," Alice said quietly. "I expect he'll forget."

I would tell David later how the shadows fell on her hair and burned the red away. Just like the hawk, Alice had hung on the air currents as long as was necessary.

Thom turned his head as we came into the house. "Will you make the coffee, Alice?" He passed through to the deck with a plate of leftovers in his hand. "The possums come up on the deck about this time of night," he explained. "Cheeky young devils will take whatever you give them."

Later, we took our coffee out to the deck. Thom settled on the wicker sofa with Alice beside him; David and I took the two chairs across from them. Alice shook off her sandals and swung her feet up on to Thom's lap. He looked at her in surprise, then rested his hand lightly on the tanned skin of her feet.

At that moment I wanted the romance of a grotto, an elegant sundial, the high stone wall. "How would a sunken garden look behind our house?" I asked David.

"You don't need it, Kate," Alice said quickly. Her hair was dark, darker than ever, and heavy. It seemed to hold her head down against the arm of the sofa.

David smiled at me. "If Alice says we don't need it, we don't need it." I saw the same lopsided grin on David's face that all our boys had and I wondered if David would hold my feet in the same way if I suddenly lifted them into his lap?

Alice leaned back. Thom slid his fingers around the arch of her foot. "The possums will come soon," she said, her voice barely a whisper.

Dingo Lad

Bennie Marsh headed down the back lane. He liked the quiet of the dirt roads and how the moths swarmed the street lights. Bennie had slipped out of the house while his father and older brother watched World Wide Wrestling on television, before his brother could use him to practice headlocks. He came to Ellen's window and saw she was sitting on the bed reading her *Films Today* magazine, light hair, white skin, the blinds open. Ellen was beautiful. One moment she was short and scrawny, messy hair, then like Cinderella hit by the magic wand, she was changed. She'd ask him, "Do you like this lipstick?" pouting her lips. Next, she was kicking him on the shins, saying, "Get away from me!"

He moved away from the window in case she caught him. Once before she'd thrown a sneaker through the open window. He didn't want her angry with him again. "You're such a dillbrain, Bennie," she'd said. "Grow up!"

A possum scooted across the road, paws scrabbling on the ashphalt and Bennie moved down by the fence alongside Tompkins' cottage. Someone cursed and Bennie moved closer. Tompkins was walking toward the wood heap at the back of his yard, carrying a torch and shovel. His billygoat, tied to the big pine tree, snorted, dragging its chain across the ground as the links rattled.

Bennie didn't move. He was a dingo, patiently waiting. "Dingo." That's what the school kids called him. He could mimic bird sounds—cockatoos, kookaburras, currawongs—but one day a kid asked him to howl like a dingo cornered by a kangaroo. He imagined the roos' hind foot with its razor-sharp claw readied, felt the pain in his gut and let out a long, wrenching howl that stunned them. "That sure was a dingo howl!" the kids chorused and the nickname stuck.

"Quiet, you old bastard," Tompkins' flashlight lit up the yellow eyes of the goat. Its chain rattled.

Bennie held his breath in fear he'd been heard but after a few moments Tompkins began pacing. One, two, three, four. Tompkins started digging. The shovel struck metal. He dug around the sound, not a large hole, so whatever he was after was not set deep in the earth.

In the light of the torch, Bennie saw a dirt-caked Nestle's Powdered Milk tin, one of those big ones. Tompkins took a short-handled screwdriver from his pocket and levered up the lid. It was full of bills. Tompkins took a handful of money from his coat pocket and stuffed it in the tin. He put the tin back in the hole, took up his shovel and spread the dirt. Bennie had heard gossip about Tompkins being a greedy old fart. What would Ellen say when he told her? He couldn't believe his good fortune.

Tompkins moved round the woodheap and started digging again. Bennie edged down the fence when Tompkins' torch flashed skyward, toward him. The billygoat's chain rattled. Bennie lay down beside a thorny bush and pressed his face to the ground, dingo-like. He heard Tompkins beat the ground with the shovel then his footsteps shuffle back over the grass toward the house.

Bennie waited outside the diner for Ellen to finish her shift. He could see her flipping burgers, cutting lettuce, wiping her sweaty forehead with the back of her sleeve. She wore clear plastic gloves that glistened. "They stop germs from spreading," Ellen had told him. He saw her clean down the cook top, throw the paper towels in the trash. She said something to her friend, Patsy, and they both laughed while she took off her apron and cap. The money was there for the taking. Would Ellen go away with him if he had a lot of money? She'd said once, "You know, Bennie, this is one, lousy, half-horse town! I want some excitement!" With Tompkin's money they could take off for Sydney or Melbourne. They'd have a holiday, visit the beaches; he could see Ellen's long white legs in a bathing suit. He thought of the money in his hands, of the possibilities, of the little blue Morris Minor sitting on the lot at Stowe's Used Cars. He worked with his dad and older brother installing windows and blowing insulation into people's attic and his dad didn't pay much.

"I'm off now," she called to her boss. Bennie didn't like Harold King, the way he stood close to Ellen when they talked. Harold was full of it. He squeezed every last penny out of the diner; went to Queensland with his wife for holidays, left Ellen to run things so he didn't see her for days.

"Hey, Ellen," Bennie called as she came through the door, waving good-bye to Patsy, gathering up her handbag. Patsy was a heavy girl, with stocky legs. She and Ellen shared scarves and jewelry, painted each other's nails, fingers and toes. Patsy had an older brother, Cliff, who worked in Hudson's Garage. He could take a car apart and put it back together over a weekend. Bennie didn't like the way Cliff teased Ellen when they were all together and she laughed up in his face.

"I'm tired, Bennie, go away," Ellen examined her nail polish.

"I've got something to tell you, something real important." He hurried after her. He hated how he sounded out of breath.

"Not tonight, Bennie!"

"I've found some money," he said. "Lots of money!"

Ellen stopped. "What are you talking about?"

Bennie put his hands in his pockets. "I was out walking last night and saw old Tompkins in his backyard," he said. "He was digging holes and burying his money."

"How much money, Bennie?" She looked more beautiful than usual.

"Lots."

She walked toward the metal seat by the corner bus stop. When she sat, he sat beside her. Not touching. He could smell the stale oil they used at the diner for frying potato chips.

"I'll have to think about this," Ellen said.

"What's to think about?"

"Walk me home, Bennie. Tell me more."

Bennie told her about the Nestle's Powdered Milk tin filled with different colored dollar notes and explained the billygoat's noisy chain.

"We can go off together," he said shyly. "Just you and me."

"I've always wanted to leave here. Go to the city." She sighed. "I'll have to plan, Bennie, I have to think it all through."

"There's money enough," he said.

"I'm glad you told me, Bennie." Ellen's hair was straw-colored, her eyes dark. They reached her house and she touched his hand. "Meet me at the diner on Saturday. I'm off at five."

Bennie knew Ellen would make a plan. She was smart.

On Saturday, Bennie walked into the diner and sat in a booth by the door.

Ellen waved as she took off her apron and cap, both stamped in green letters with Harry's Diner. It was still light outside but people were coming in for an early supper.

"Patsy can leave early today," Ellen said.

Bennie didn't want Patsy in on the plan. He knew the girls had been friends forever but he wanted it to be just the two of them, Ellen and him.

"Hiyah, Dingo." Patsy gave Bennie's arm a little punch. "Hear you've got something exciting to tell us?"

They walked out the door in single file, Bennie last. The two girls sat together on the metal seat by the bus stop. Bennie stood near Ellen.

"We need Patsy," Ellen said. "If the plan's going to work, we'll need three of us. There's the goat to worry about."

"Okay," he said.

"Bennie you bring a shovel." Bennie shifted his feet. "Patsy, you'll need gloves." Patsy nodded.

"I have a canvas bag to put the tins in," Ellen added. "And a torch."

"You sure you can keep the goat quiet?" Bennie asked Patsy.

Patsy giggled. "Goats don't scare me none. I'm going to hold the old bugger while you and Ellen dig."

"We do it tonight," Ellen said. "After Tompkins goes to the pub." Bennie rubbed his hands together. Patsy grinned. "Nine o'clock it should be dark enough," Ellen said. "We'll meet by his back fence." She and Patsy linked arms and started walking. "Patsy's going to wait at my house, Bennie. Okay?"

It wasn't okay to just leave him behind. He could have walked Ellen to her door. Patsy knew her way home. "Okay," said Bennie.

At nine, he met the girls at Tomkins back fence. They both had on long dark jackets, hair tied in pony tails, dark shoes. Bennie wore his black sweater and dark sweats. The clothes he wore when he went walking at night. What if he couldn't remember where Tomkins had been digging and Ellen laughed at him. Patsy would make fun of him, too. "Gee, Dingo, still can't keep anything straight," she'd say. Maybe Ellen would defend him. Sometimes she did.

Bennie pushed through the broken slats in the fence, followed by Ellen. Patsy caught her ankle and Ellen helped her through. A light shone in the house. Maybe Tompkins hadn't gone to the pub, maybe he was home watching the telly. The billygoat bleated and rattled its chain.

Ellen put her finger to her lips. She switched on her torch and caught the goat's yellow eyes. She quickly turned the beam on the ground around the woodheap. Patsy walked over to the goat, making soft shushing sounds while Bennie searched for odd mounds of leaves, tamped down grass. He spotted a likely place and brought the edge of the shovel down hard.

Metal on metal! He wanted to whoop. Ellen came over with the torch. He dug around like Tomkins had, sweating. There was a Nestle's tin. He continued around the woodheap, poking the shovel into the soil, until he found the other tin. Ellen held the torch steady on the two dirt-covered tins while Patsy held the goat's chain and talked to it softly.

Bennie held up the tins, "These are the two he put money in."

Ellen pulled a metal spoon from her pocket and prized off one of the lids. The money was clear to see, poking up stiffly through the opening.

"Make sure you spread some leaves," Ellen said as she closed the lid. "We don't want Tomkins to find his money gone right away, do we?" He had to lean in to hear her. She still smelled like frying oil and lavender.

Bennie went back round the woodheap, spreading leaves and woodchips, tamping down soil. When he finished Ellen caught his arm, "You did great, Bennie," she said. Her eyes shone, her lips were dark red. "We'll have fun spending it all, won't we?" She laughed softly and spun round to take Patty's hand.

The goat pulled at its chain, wanting to follow Patsy. "Come on, Bennie," Ellen called, already at the fence. She dropped the torch into her bag and it clinked against the metal tins.

"We'll catch the early train?" Bennie whispered, bending close to her ear. "Just you and me?"

"I'll count the money tonight, see how much we have." Ellen said as she swung the bag onto her shoulder. "I'll divide it up, three ways, okay?"

"Can't we do it together?" Bennie asked.

"Patsy and I can do it." Ellen's face was drained of color. "We're good at math, Bennie, you know that" She shifted the canvas bag to her other shoulder. "Come on, Patsy, I'm getting cold."

He wanted to be there when they did the sharing. He had a suitcase packed and ready. There was only the early train on Sundays. "You'll bring it tomorrow? To the station?" He looked at Ellen and she nodded.

"Seeya, Dingo," Patsy called. The two girls disappeared between the bushes. There were lights in her house so her parents were home; it was late but she was good with excuses. She could always say Harold kept them over to clean up.

Bennie slipped through his front door and passed the living room. The TV was off. He'd avoided another wrestling match with his brother. "Gotta learn the moves, Dingo," his brother would say, punching his arm. "Gotta grow up!" When he got to Sydney he'd call his brother. "You'll never guess where I am?" he'd say. And he'd wait for his brother to suck in his breath before he told him.

But he'd done it! He'd found the money. He'd take Ellen away. Surely there'd be enough money for meals and hotels and train fares, with extra for him since he'd made the discovery? He imagined himself in the little blue Morris, windows down. He'd go to Hudson's Garage with his pockets full of money and he'd bargain with Cliff for an overhaul even though he didn't trust him. He had no choice; Hudson's was the only garage in town.

At the train station, he tightened his grip on the suitcase. The sun wasn't up yet but the white walls of the station were stark in the half light.

Bennie checked his watch. The train was due any minute. Where was Ellen?

"Where're you going?" Mr. Bradley asked from behind the grille at the ticket window. "You need to buy a ticket, can't go for free."

"I'm waiting for a friend," Bennie said. "We're going to Sydney. On a holiday."

"Train will be here soon," the ticket master tapped the counter. "Make up your mind."

Bennie watched the rising mist off Broad Pond. He felt in his empty pockets. He could try and hold the train for her; he knew he could if she was running up the road, if she was only a little late. He squinted, trying to spot her grey coat and green scarf.

The train's whistle blew behind him.

Bennie put his suitcase on the ground. Damn them! He knew he shouldn't have trusted Patsy. Where was Ellen? She had promised. His body filled with pain. He remembered his brother's words, "Gotta grow up, Bennie, gotta learn about the world!" He was the dingo once again, knowing his fate, afraid. Bennie began shaking. He held his stomach tightly and bent over his folded arms. What a dillbrain he'd been.

He howled so long and hard Mr. Bradley flew out from his ticket window.

"You alright, son?" he asked.

But Bennie couldn't answer. From the platform he could see the tall neon lights of Stowe's Used Cars where the little blue Morris sat waiting, and beyond those lights the black and white sign for Hudson's Garage.

Currawongs

In those first warm months of '44, while the new season's crops were planted, dozens of men drifted south from Sydney, discharged soldiers mostly, ordinary men who arrived home from the war filled with hope and glory only to find their world had changed.

"They're after work. Something to eat," Carrie's father told her as he dug the new garden.

"Where do the tramps go?" Carrie asked.

Her father brought the mattock down hard on a clump of matted roots. "They walk where the rabbits run, along the side of the fences. And they go where the rabbits go through the holes in the netting." He was preparing a new garden bed for the house vegetables, the barrow beside him filled with compost and soil and packets of seeds. "Some will settle, some won't," he said as he made a furrow to receive the seeds.

Carrie was reminded of the currawongs that flew into the gully the summer before she turned eleven. A flock of them came, twenty or thirty crowbirds, and they settled in the topmost branches of the gum trees. She had never seen so many before. "Bush fires burned out their feeding grounds," her father had explained. "It's forced them south." The currawongs swooped over the farm, and up, circling the paddocks and ploughed ground, at times flying so close Carrie saw their sharp beaks open and close on their cries.

Only two tramps stayed longer than a night, the others accepted some food, slept in the shed, and were gone on the road by morning. The first to stay was a wrinkled old man with his hair tied back by a piece of string and his trousers held by a length of rope looped in a sailor's knot. He came through early in the day. He was tired, he said, but his hands were good for a bit of work, his legs were still strong, though he'd never worked on the land before. "It'll be sweet to sleep under some shelter," he told Carrie. "The roads get long after a time."

The old tramp played a mouth organ, marching songs and hymns and sad little melodies that kept Carrie from sleeping that night. She heard her mother pacing in the corner bedroom before the window closed with a snap, but Carrie listened on, wondering where all the tunes came from, where he carried them, where he'd heard them before.

"Let him stay," her mother said next morning. "He can chop some wood, mend the back fence."

Her father looked up from his mug of tea.

"Something?" she asked.

"We can't pay them."

"We can feed them." Her mother pushed the saucepan of beef dripping to the back of the stove and checked the pot of chicken broth.

"The tramps are all men." Carrie said to her mother as they moved into the bedroom. "Where are the women?"

"It's not easy on the roads."

"And the children?"

Her mother floated a clean sheet over the bed. "In the city, poor things."

"Do the men go back?" Carrie asked.

"I don't know." Her mother tucked the thin grey blankets tightly under the horse-hair mattress. "Maybe some do."

The next evening, the old tramp played his mouth organ, and instead of going to bed, Carrie and her parents sat on the verandah and listened. Her mother held an ivory fan with a bow of white satin tied through the handle. She fanned herself slowly, and the ivory blades clacked at each sweep. "Isn't that *Over There?*" she asked, and, "I believe that's *Pack Up Your Troubles in Your Old Kit Bag.*"

"*Night and Day,*" her father answered after a pause. He sat on the edge of the verandah, legs stretched down the front steps, boots crossed on each other, a cigarette in his hand.

Her mother snorted. "You don't know one tune from another."

"I like them slow," he said.

"Rubbish!" she answered.

"I know what I like."

"Once," she replied, "you liked them fast." She flicked her fan shut and held it to her lips.

"There you go." He looked around and smiled at Carrie. "Can't best your mother when it comes to music."

They had a radio that worked when the batteries were charged, but they didn't have a piano like the Pomeroys or a player like the McGraths. Her mother sang the songs she knew, but her voice would give out on a run of high notes, and she'd laugh and begin again. She sang parts of a song over and over, sometimes only the refrain, until the few lines of melody looped endlessly in Carrie's head.

"Where do all the songs come from?" Carrie asked the old tramp while he chopped the wood. His knuckles were large and shiny.

"The city," he said. "You been there?"

"No," Carrie shook her head and picked up the wood pieces. She threw them into the wheelbarrow with the others.

"You have a wireless?" he asked.

"Sometimes the batteries go dead."

"Then you'll have to go to Sydney when you grow up." The old tramp said. "Go to the theater, that's where the music plays like something out of your dreams." He paused in his chopping, left the axe in the log and rubbed his hands. "I remember the Royal," he said. "There was a curtain draped across the stage, crimson plush, with a golden fringe that swept the stage when it opened. Everything was gold. The chandeliers sparkled like they were made of ice—take your breath away. There were cupids in every nook and corner with little wings." Carrie sat next to the tramp on one of the logs, the axe leaned against her knee. "The gents and ladies sailed down the aisle in clothes you couldn't imagine, decked out in jewels and furs fit to beat the band."

"A hush comes." He painted the air with his hands. "The lights dim, and the orchestra begins to play. They play the curtain up, and up, to the very roof."

Carrie heard the humming silence of the grand audience. "Did you go often?"

"I played the clarinet," he sighed. "I came back home with my lips soft and my fingers stiff." He took up the axe again, and the chips didn't fly so high.

The next day he was gone, the tramp and his music.

"He earned his keep," her mother said. But it was days before she sang again.

Another tramp came through, a younger man who limped and had three fingers on his right hand. Carrie saw her mother talking to him on the verandah. Her hands were rolled in her apron until she touched his arm. She asked him to stay for afternoon tea, and he sat at the kitchen table, the only tramp invited into the house.

Her mother poured from the brown teapot, tipping it so the tea leaves brewed nice and strong. She put her chin in her hands as she listened to the young man, and her face lit up with the questions she had.

"Did you know him?" Carrie asked later while her mother ironed the clothes on the kitchen table.

"He came from Wagga," her mother said. "Three streets over from where I was born." She paused. "He knew the Brackett and Thomas boys. He told me Jimmy Brackett died in France and Hap Thomas was taken prisoner. We were all such friends then." She set the iron on its edge. "He used to swim in the river, the same swimming hole we did." She turned Carrie's blue skirt and smoothed the pleats with her hand. "He's on his way home now."

"Why?" Carrie asked.

"He hasn't learned to manage his right hand yet." Her mother ran the iron smoothly up the flattened pleats.

Only last week, Carrie had worn this blue skirt her mother was ironing to the dance at the church hall. Cy Dunning had played the fiddle there, and Bertha Green the piano. The lights in the rafters had caught Cy's gold armbands, glowed off the white silk handkerchief he placed between his chin and the polished wood of his fiddle. "*Canadian Three-Step!*" He'd called to the packed hall. "*Gypsy Tap! Snowball!*"

Carrie had watched her parents dance; her mother's palm rested on her father's shoulder while his large hand covered the little buttons on the back of her best dress. Her mother's face was soft and flushed, and they did the same steps together without ever faltering.

Carrie danced with Barbara and Margaret in the shadows of the hall, until Cy called, "*The Barn Dance!*" and for the first time her father walked the length of the hall in his double-breasted wedding suit.

"May I have the pleasure?" He asked, as solemn as when he fixed the broken hinge on the front gate. Margaret giggled, but Carrie saw her mother smile as she and her father swept by in the swell of a thousand violins.

One tramp showed Carrie how to shoot a marble off the first knuckle of her thumb with a deadly spin. He drew a big circle in the dirt with the heel of his boot and Carrie dropped her five marbles in the center of it. From his pocket he drew a large glass taw, nicked and smoky from use. The tramp crouched on the ground beside her, steadied his hand, and shot his taw into her marbles so they scattered. He picked each one off and sent them flying.

"I carried it through France," he said, rolling the taw in his fingers. "Best lucky charm a man could have." He was on his way to the city to look for a job, he said, and he needed all the luck he could get.

Carrie asked her mother, "Will I go to the city?"

"You're too young to think of those things," her mother pressed a skinned rabbit into the mound of flour and set it in a baking dish. "It's hard in the city now."

"But, it won't always be hard," Carrie said. She imagined the red velvet curtain rising to the ceiling, heard the clarinet. "Not forever, it won't."

The tall tramp was crouched beside the big gum at the second dip in the road when she walked home from school. He was dusty black—coat, pants, boots. But his hat was one of the old army ones of khaki felt with the side turned up and the brass badge of the Rising Sun pinned to the band.

"Missy," he called. Her heart beat faster than her footsteps. He called again and stood unsteadily, leaning on the flat of the tree trunk; a blanket roll rested on his shoulders. Her mother had explained that the tramps wouldn't hurt her, "Just walk by them quickly and don't stare."

They were in the kitchen, eating supper, when the tramp knocked at their door that night, standing off from the light of the hurricane lamp with his hat on his head, his hands hooked in the lapels of his coat.

"Some job I can do, mister?" he asked Carrie's father. Carrie saw him straighten his back and adjust his hat.

"Have you eaten?" her father asked, and the tramp lowered his head. "Fetch some food, Carrie."

Carrie ladled the sweet-smelling stew into a kitchen plate, cut some bread and made a mug of tea. The man accepted it with an upward glance. He was taller than her father, even on the bottom step. "You can sleep in the shed," her father said. "I'll show you where." The tramp took the food and followed her father down the yard.

"Another of them, sick," her father said when he returned. "Consumption, I'd say."

Her mother shook her head. "If it's that, we'd better be careful around him." She scalded the plate and mug he'd used and placed them apart on the shelf. "It will be difficult having him around," she said. "He makes me uneasy."

"I could do with the help," her father said.

The first morning the tramp slept in the shed, Carrie moved carefully to the bails where Maisie stood waiting. She held the handle away from the milk bucket so the metal chink wouldn't waken him. She wiped over Maisie's full udder with warm water, pressed her forehead into the warm depression in the animal's flank.

Her father came down to the shed while Carrie milked. The cow struggled a little as she heard his familiar footsteps, whisked her tail across Carrie's back. She heard the two men talking; the tramp's voice was thick, as if heavy dust clogged his throat.

"The horses died under us," she heard the tramp tell her father. "Screaming and kicking, and their blood spilled over our hands." His voice rose. "What bastards could do that? Shoot a horse out from under a man?" He coughed.

"It must have been hell, a war like that," her father answered quietly.

"Farmers were right lucky," the thin tramp said. "There were no excuses for us city men. No reason to stay behind."

Their voices faded as they moved out of the shed.

He brought the water up from the well like a bird with a broken wing, hunched, shielding his chest. He stood away from them, careful to cough off to the side, and he never took off his hat.

The next day the sky was overcast, the clouds low and black when Carrie hurried home from school. The currawongs flew before the storm, sweeping up from the gully with their fierce lonely cries to settle in the topmost branches of the eucalypts. Thunder would come soon, Carrie knew, then the flashes of lightning and the first great drops of rain to strip the leaves away. She hurried along the road until she saw the thin tramp standing at the corner of the north paddock. He was mending the corner post where one of the big horses had scratched his back so hard the fence gave way.

"Coming home, little missy?"

Carrie felt his eyes could see through the brim of his hat when his head was down, that his eyes were watching.

"You talking to me today?" The tramp wiped his mouth with his coat sleeve and leaned on the shovel handle. He coughed, gathering phlegm in his mouth and spat off to the side.

Carrie stayed in the middle of the road. She smelled the storm clouds gathering overhead. "It's going to rain real soon," she said.

"Rain don't bother me none." Sweat dripped off his chin.

"You've got to be careful of the lightning here." She would talk for a bit, but she'd keep her distance. "I heard you talking about the war. About the horses dying." She shifted the straps of her schoolbag.

"Anything dies, it's hard." He lay down the shovel and picked up the hoop of fencing wire, pulling the strand out so it curled on the ground. "Seen too much dying."

Carrie stared at him. "Have you been in a theater?" she asked. "With an orchestra?"

"Orchestra?" He spat off to the side. "You're a nosy little thing." He sent a shovel full of dirt into the trough around the post.

"Playing music?" she continued.

"Rattle of dice? Sound of two-bobs smacking the ground? I reckon you don't mean that, now do you, little missy?" He laughed, and shook his hand as though he was playing craps.

Maybe he didn't know the old tramp's city where people sang in another language and the music told a story. Carrie remembered his words: It makes you laugh and it makes you cry, it's life, you understand?

"I'm not talking about games." She started walking.

"Hold on!" he called. "Why you asking?"

How could she find words to put around it? "Someone told me about Sydney, and the Royal Theater. The music. How there was an orchestra and a conductor in white gloves. He told me the women wore feathers in their hair."

The tramp held the hoop of wire against his chest. "Go on," he said. The first large drops of rain fell on his hat and the shoulders of his black coat.

"The old man played a clarinet in the orchestra." She lifted her head, and the rain fell on her cheeks, spattered her schoolbag.

"Whoever it was told you that, is having you on." He pulled more wire from the hoop. "Only theaters I know, people use for a bit of a doss. You know what I mean?"

"He lost his music in the war."

"He was lucky." The tramp poked the wire through the post hole while the rain fell on the newly tamped earth at his feet. "You lose more than music in a flaming war." He coughed thickly and spat into the rain.

"He still has it," Carrie said. "He keeps it in a special case lined with blue silk."

"You see this badge here?" He pointed to his hat. "This digger's medal? This Rising Sun's all I've got from the war." He twisted the wire ends together. "Nothing more than a lousy piece of brass!"

He turned the hammer in the second wire loop. His hands slipped and the hammer spun upwards with a crack, into his face. "StruthJeesus!" He dropped to the ground and rocked back to rest on his heels. He covered his cheek with his hand, and a trickle of blood ran from his nose and gathered on his upper lip.

"Help me up!" he called. His hand reaching for hers was streaked with earth and blood. Carrie backed away. There was a roll of thunder that roused the currawongs from the trees, and cawing loudly, they flew in a black cloud for the shelter of the gully. "You gonna just walk away?" he called again. His hat lay on the ground beside his knee, his hair was matted. He wiped the blood off his chin and his voice was cold and mean. "Let me tell you, little Missy, there's no music like you're talking about. Not in any city, anywhere in the world."

"You're a liar," Carrie whispered. It was too late to beat the storm. "A liar!" She ran down the road with her schoolbag bumping on her shoulders, the rain striking her face. "I'm going to get to the Royal Theater," she shouted as she pushed open the front gate. "And I'm going to hear that music one day."

Acknowledgments

I grew up on a small farm named Girrawheen (an Aboriginal name meaning "place of flowers") some 70 odd miles southwest of Sydney, Australia. Mine was a happy carefree childhood, rather lonely, but invigorated by short visits to relatives in Sydney. My father taught me to love that farm, my mother taught me to look beyond its boundaries.

This book of short stories has been a long time coming. I started crafting stories when I began a Master in Fine Arts in Writing at Vermont College in 1987. Now, 30 years later, a book has formed. Many of these stories flow from fragmented memories drawn from the forties and fifties post-war years in Australia.

I would like to thank Joni Beth Cole for her rousing encouragement, Deb Heimann for her eye for detail, and Deborah McKew for her editing and publishing skills. Thank you to Matteo Grillis, wildlife painter and blogger, for his beautiful butcher bird watercolors.

CPSIA information can be obtained at www.ICGtesting.com
Printed in the USA
BVOW01s0034270816

459980BV00002B/5/P

9 781934 582725